"You are judging me without knowing what drives me,"

Jeremiah stated. "You have not given me a chance since the very first time we met, have you? You are afraid of commitments, Sarah. That is what this boils down to."

"That is not true."

"You are too afraid that what we share now might grow into something significant, are you not?"

Sarah dropped her gaze to the floor. Her heart twisted in the wrong direction, hurting much as it had when renegades had killed her husband. That couldn't be. There was only one man she loved that much, and his name was not Jeremiah Stewart.

TAMMY SHUTTLESWORTH is a native of Ohio who now resides in Haughton, Louisiana with her husband and two daughters. She retired from the air force and now teaches Junior ROTC classes to the LA801st Wing at Haughton High School. Besides novels, she writes short stories and poetry. Her first two books were inspired by the rich Ohio history she grew up hearing about and exploring.

Books by Tammy Shuttleworth

HEARTSONG PRESENTS
HP308—A Different Kind of Heaven

Healing
Sarah's Heart

Tammy Shuttlesworth

Heartsong Presents

This story is dedicated to the memory of those Christian Indians who died in the 1782 Gnadenhutten Massacre, Gnadenhutten, Ohio. May their souls rest in eternal peace.

My thanks to Becky Germany for giving me the original idea for this story. To my husband, Rick, who believed I could do it—I love you. And a special thanks to the Great Physician, who heals all hearts, if we ask.

A note from the author:
I love to hear from my readers! You may correspond with me by writing: **Tammy Shuttlesworth**
Author Relations
PO Box 719
Uhrichsville, OH 44683

ISBN 1-57748-984-5

HEALING SARAH'S HEART

All of the characters and events in this book are fictitious. Any resemblance to actual persons, living or dead, or to actual events is purely coincidental.

Cover illustration by Jocelyn Bouchard.

PRINTED IN THE U.S.A.

one

"I hope this brings better news than the last one did, sir." Jeremiah handed the pouch across the table, watching anxiously as David Williamson unraveled the leather straps.

Williamson's dark eyes perused the missive before turning to Jeremiah. "It is times like these when men are asked to give more than they planned."

"I did not think it would be good tidings when I picked up the message at Fort Pitt," Jeremiah replied.

"You are right. This brings news of another attack."

Jeremiah continually hoped the need for their group of defenders would fade. But there was no indication that would happen. Though Washington County had abundant steeply sloped hills, gently gurgling streams, and quiet meadows, it also was within easy reach of Indians, who crossed the Ohio River to rid themselves of their frustrations.

"I was afraid of that, sir," Jeremiah said. "How far away was this one?"

"About a two-day ride. This reinforces our need to find more men and to ensure they are ready to fight." Williamson paused. "Despite your insistence to the contrary, you do know that you are a great help to our cause."

Jeremiah shifted from foot to foot. "I do my part, sir, but you know my view on killing."

"I would never ask you to do something I would not do myself," the colonel assured him. "But the fact is, things are getting worse."

Jeremiah motioned to the dispatch. "What happened this time?"

Williamson gave a deep sigh. "Last week, on April nineteenth, General Brodhead attacked an Indian camp near the head of the Muskingum River. He suspected they were British allies."

Jeremiah scrubbed a hand back and forth across his neck. "Suspecting and knowing are two different things."

Williamson nodded. "Yes. Well, he went south to Fort Henry before he headed to Ohio and ended up with more than three hundred men on his side. According to this, the Muskingum River was high due to recent heavy rains, with half the tribe on the other side. The general did not capture all the prisoners he wanted. He did manage to corral twenty men, women, and children and forced them to march upriver. His men massacred the hostages not far from the fort."

"Massacred them! Did he not think about the consequences of that action?"

"Apparently the general is not one to concern himself greatly with such things," Williamson said in a carefully controlled tone. "Since we are so close to Fort Pitt, I think we need to prepare for retaliation."

"I wish there were another way to resolve this situation," Jeremiah answered. "I know warriors destroy families, burn crops, and terrorize innocent children. And I know I should be glad to halt such atrocities, yet—"

"Almost everyone in these parts believes the Wyandots are responsible for the raids," Williamson interrupted. "But I am not so sure. Something must have made the general think that he needed to attack that Delaware tribe."

"I have ridden through that part of Ohio," Jeremiah pointed out. "Some of the Indians there are led by Moravian missionaries. They call themselves Praying Indians. We cannot blame a tribe for something they may not have done."

"You know what it is like to lose a family member,"

Williamson responded. "Revenge often comes before rational thought. I am afraid it will not take much to get the men of *this* county thinking along those lines."

"That does not mean I have to like it," Jeremiah declared.

"No, but it is becoming a fact of life," Williamson said. "While I believe that if we were able to get that British commander at Fort Detroit to quit inciting the redskins we might have a chance at some peace and quiet, it does not seem likely that will occur."

Jeremiah placed his hands on the back of the chair in front of him. He'd ridden nonstop for two days. His back ached from the jarring motion of his horse. He wanted nothing more than a hot meal and a long night's sleep.

"There are other Indian groups in that area," Jeremiah offered. "Besides the Christian Delawares, there is a group of Mohicans. I cannot see why you think they would be responsible for the assaults."

Williamson narrowed his eyes. "I know you do not believe in violence, Jeremiah. But is that all that bothers you about this?"

Jeremiah wanted no part of killing. That was why he had considered asking Williamson to relieve him of his militia position.

"Well?" Williamson challenged. "The sooner you get it out in the open, the sooner we can deal with it."

Doom echoed in Jeremiah's heart, much as it had the night he lost Jenny. He studied the man who he knew bore the responsibility for more than two hundred lives on his shoulders. Williamson's hair and brows were a prematurely grizzled gray, and weariness filled his eyes.

"How is the muster going?" Jeremiah asked, diverting the conversation.

"Last count showed eighty dependable men," Williamson

bragged. "But while you were gone, another family was attacked. It will not be the last," he added. "The redcoats will prod until they get the warriors to chase us out of here. I wish we were not so close to the Ohio River."

"We are farther east than some," Jeremiah replied, thinking again about how Indians had disrupted his own life.

"Distance will not keep our kinfolk safe," Williamson argued. "Those warriors ride till they see a home, then they strike. You know what is left when they finish."

Jeremiah wished he'd dropped off the missive and gone to his cabin. The tiny house nestled in the hills had been empty when Jeremiah arrived in Washington County. He knew why but tried not to let that bother him.

Williamson drummed his fingers on the desk. "We are going to have to take drastic measures, whether we want to or not."

"Are you sure that is wise?"

"Being in command sometimes means ignoring what others think," Williamson replied. "The settlers did not elect me because I would make everyone happy. They put me here because they trusted me to do a good job."

"Of course, sir, but—"

"They expect me to protect them," Williamson went on, seemingly oblivious to Jeremiah's anxiety. "That means I have only one choice—to go out on the trail and see for myself what is happening."

"You mentioned earlier that Major Whelp is out on patrol," Jeremiah said. "If you go, there will be no one left in charge."

"Every good leader does need a dependable backup." Williamson clasped his hands in front of him on the desk.

"So you will wait until Major Whelp returns?"

Williamson studied his hands. "You know I have a very high regard for you."

Jeremiah nodded. "You are one of the few who do not hold

my past against me, sir. I appreciate that."

Williamson waved a hand in the air. "We all make mistakes. I have made plenty in my day. But what I am about to tell you is no mistake." Williamson gazed at Jeremiah. "I signed you up as a county lieutenant. I know you will do a good job."

Jeremiah bounded from behind the chair. "With all due respect, sir, you cannot do that. I promised to serve as a courier. Nothing more."

Williamson gave him a pointed look. "May I remind you that since I am in charge, I can do whatever I wish? The subject is closed."

"But, sir," Jeremiah began, ready to protest this unexpected turn of events.

It was no use. Williamson had turned to examine a map on the wall. There was only one thing left to do, a habit from as far back as Jeremiah could recall.

Lord, I know I forgot to thank You for bringing me back safely on this ride. Please accept my gratitude now. If it wasn't for You, I wouldn't accomplish the things I do. I know You've led me down some strange paths before. . .but, Lord? I don't like the looks of this.

"Lieutenant Stewart!" The colonel's smile was broader than the gate leading into Jeremiah's family's pasture, showing his obvious pleasure with Jeremiah's promotion. "I like the sound of that title. How about you?"

"I do not think this is a good idea," Jeremiah spoke candidly. "Major Whelp will not be happy."

"I knew you would be. . .well, should we say less than enthusiastic?" Williamson consoled. "This is only temporary. One hundred eighty days. Come on, Jeremiah. You are one of the few people in this county who can read and write, and the men trust you."

"But what about Major Whelp?" Jeremiah repeated. "No matter what I do, he does not like me."

Williamson snorted. "Whelp could not find a teepee if someone placed his hands on either side of its entrance. He is second in command only because he finished behind me in the election." He pointed to a map on the wall. "Pay close attention, Stewart. This is what you need to know to catch up on what has been going on around here." The colonel began to point out different areas on the map.

Aren't you even going to protest? a little voice in Jeremiah's mind asked.

Jeremiah frowned. No one argued with Williamson and won. He doubted that even the Almighty could change the colonel's mind once it was made up—the stubborn streak in the Williamson family was as long as the Ohio River.

It was late April. Six months would take him to December. Did the one hundred eighty days start today? Or tomorrow?

two

"I think this is the most beautiful country I have ever seen," Bessie Hall said with a sigh.

Sarah Lyons turned to the woman she had traveled with for seventy miles. Bessie's curly red hair tumbled about her face, but her sparkling green eyes reflected her delight.

Bessie is the closest thing to a friend I have, Sarah reminded herself. *I must be pleasant.*

"It is green for September," Sarah agreed. "I am so glad the nights of having to stay alert are over." Sarah stretched to work out the cramps in her lower back that had accumulated with the miles.

"We made it. That is the important thing," Bessie said.

Despair swamped Sarah's heart as she watched Bessie caress a wilted sprig of late-blooming posies that her husband had tucked at her bosom.

Levi will never bring me *flowers again,* Sarah thought. Yet she strove to sound unaffected. "I am still amazed your husband let you travel."

"You know how strongly Captain believes in the power of prayer," Bessie said. "He was convinced that we had to be here now."

Sarah prayed occasionally, but it had been a long time since she'd believed God answered her prayers.

"He trusted God to bring us here safely," Bessie continued, looking around. "We made it, Sarah. We really made it!"

"So we did," Sarah replied with little excitement. No matter how important this move was for her son's future, her feelings about it were as dismal as the mud-covered moccasins she stared at.

"And Samuel did not give you any of the trouble that you feared he would, Sarah. That is one fine boy you are raising. I hope my children turn out to be as mannerly as he. You must be proud of him."

Sarah glanced at her four year old, Sammy, who was nestled in a corner of the wagon. His thumb hovered near the "o" of his mouth. Shafts of sunlight highlighted his auburn hair. Others called him Samuel, but to Sarah and Levi he was "Sammy." Sarah hoped Sammy turned out to be a fine young man. She owed it to Levi to raise their son the best she could.

Bessie's chatter drew Sarah's attention. "I wish Captain would get back. I wonder why he did not want us going in the house with him?"

Sarah didn't answer; she just glanced about them. They had stopped their wagon not far from some dilapidated structures. Sarah became nervous in places she wasn't familiar with—she hoped Captain would return soon.

"I do so hope our home is ready," Bessie went on. "I am glad the colonel found a circuit opening for Captain. He might be gone when the baby comes, but Williamson is going to pay us in food and supplies. Does that bother you, Sarah?"

Sarah's jaw tightened. "You know I do not like it. Until I get my life settled I have no choice but to depend on others."

"Doing so is not that bad, Sarah. David is a good man. So many others are, too, if you would only let them prove themselves."

Sarah sighed. "I imagine so, Bessie. But right now I do not want commitments of any sort."

"I think someday you will change your mind," Bessie replied. "Oh! Did I tell you what Captain said about the militia? I cannot wait to see the men marching in their best and putting on a parade! Does that not sound exciting?"

"I did not come here to see men of any sort, those on display or otherwise," Sarah reminded Bessie.

"Perhaps not," Bessie announced. "But the people you meet here will welcome you. One day you will not hurt as much as you do now." She patted Sarah's forearm tenderly.

Sarah pulled away. She didn't want a fuss made over her.

Just then Sammy awoke. "Mama?"

Sarah smiled at her son, grateful for his intrusion. She pulled Sammy onto her lap and straightened his shirt.

"About time you arose, sleepyhead," she said, ruffling his hair. "Look! Over there is the river Captain promised we would see. And beyond those trees is where Bessie says our new home is."

Sammy glanced briefly toward the woods before turning back to her. "Go see water?"

Sarah's gaze flitted between sloppy tents and lazy horses. She must quit thinking that harm waited around every corner.

"If Bessie does not mind." She gave Bessie a questioning look.

"Go on," Bessie encouraged. "It will do you good."

Sarah swung her son off the wagon, ignoring her tears. It was silly to think that Sammy would be eager to see his new home. He was too young to realize what they'd lost.

Sammy is the only one who makes me laugh, Sarah reminded herself. *He depends on me to take care of him, to help him grow. Perhaps taking him to the river will help pass the time until Captain returns. And then. . .*

Sarah shook the thoughts away. She was just anxious to find someplace warmer to sleep than on the ground beneath the wagon. The September air in the Ohio Valley could be slightly cool or downright cold at night. Lately it had been the latter.

"Will you join us, Bessie?" Sarah asked.

"I do not think so. I will just sit here and enjoy getting kicked by this young 'un." Bessie laid her hands on her rounded abdomen. "He will only be in here a few more months. Go on, Sarah. Samuel needs some pleasure in his life right now. So do you. Nothing will happen. Captain would not have left us here if it were dangerous."

Bessie is right, Sarah advised herself. *I haven't been happy lately and it has affected Sammy. I came here with the Halls to make life better for us, so I might as well start doing so.*

Sarah folded her hand over her son's pudgy fingers and matched his small steps as they strolled toward the riverbank. Leaves rustled underfoot, the product of fall's frosty hands. A few birds swooped overhead, filling the emptiness with tiny chirps. Sammy spied some twigs on the ground and giggled as he tossed them into the river.

While the distant clang of a blacksmith's forge carried to them, a soggy mass of clouds drifted overhead. The resultant shadows filled Sarah's heart with remembrance.

It might not be a harbor in the wilderness, but I miss our home, she thought.

"Twees sleeping, Mama." Sammy pointed out a barge headed down river.

"They do look like it," she agreed. "They are taking the trees to people so that they may build houses," Sarah informed him.

Sammy jabbered some more while Sarah turned her mind back to her situation. She hadn't understood how difficult it would be to leave the area that had been her home for seven years.

She missed the land she and Levi had built a three-room home on. There were so many pretty sights—trees welcoming spring with new buds, deer coming to the natural salt lick in the valley. The trees and the deer were still there, but not their home. Sarah pushed the thought away. *Lighten your heart,* she scolded herself, *for Sammy's sake.*

"Listen, Sammy. I hear Bessie calling. Hurry now!"

Sarah chased Sammy back to the wagon, flapping her apron at him. She smiled at his squeals of joy, but as she climbed aboard behind her son, disappointment was in her eyes. Perhaps when they got settled she and Sammy would walk here. It seemed like a place of hope, of peace. Something Sarah sorely needed.

❧

"These must be read immediately, sir. Then you need to write out the requisitions for supplies. Then there is the complaint that must be handled. Now, let me think. Oh, yes. If you have any questions, the colonel said he would be back in two days. There, I think that is it."

Jeremiah stared at the stack of papers the clerk had thrust at him. "I guess that settles what I will be doing for the rest of the evening."

"Did you have other plans, sir?"

"Of course not. And please stop calling me sir. Save that for the real boss around here."

The clerk grinned. "Sure thing, Lieutenant Stewart."

❧

As they passed houses strung between trees like fallen pine cones, a variety of sights and sounds assailed Sarah. Men shouted, axes splintered firewood, venison grilled over open pits, and children rushed around. Sarah was annoyed, not at the sight of the children, but because she wasn't sure that trying to find a new life for Sammy and her was the right thing to do.

Perhaps I should have listened to my heart and kept Sammy among familiar surroundings.

And where was that? a voice in her mind taunted. *All alone in the wilderness in a burned-out shell of a home with a young child and no man to protect you?*

But at least it was ours, Sarah argued back. *Now, except for Sammy, I have nothing—no home, no husband, no life.*

There's always the Lord, Sarah. You can depend on Him.

It wasn't the taunting tone of her sadness talking; it was her husband's voice drifting to her from within the tangled mist of remembrance. Levi never stopped believing that God would take care of them, even though Sarah's faith wavered as often as the sun rose and set.

"Keep Sammy safe, Sarah," Levi implored her just before he closed his eyes for the last time. "Promise you will take him to meet my parents and your sister. Promise me. . ." Levi's words faded into the nothingness that had taken him away from her forever.

I promise, Levi, Sarah thought, renewing her pledge. She swiped at the tear trickling down her cheek. So many wrong moves, so many chances gone bad. If only. . .

Sarah turned the ache away. She couldn't think about where loving Levi had left her; it was too hard to accept, harder still to forget. And despite Bessie and Captain's best efforts, Sarah found that pain doesn't fade easily. Sometimes, no matter how often Sammy smiled at her, she wasn't sure it ever would.

three

Sarah shaded her eyes from the piercing sun so she could gaze at the shanties huddled together. A man blowing into a horn made quite a racket. She supposed it was all part of their militia practice.

The tang of sizzling bacon filled the air. Sarah's stomach growled, for she hadn't eaten much of a morning meal. However, thoughts of food did nothing to solve her dilemma. Now, which building had Bessie said was the trading post?

Scrunching her eyes shut to help her recall didn't help. She'd been in such a tizzy, with Sammy pulling at her apron while Bessie reeled off instructions, that she had failed to listen properly. At least the trail though the trees was well marked. The trading post was another matter.

Sarah stared at the building beside the one they stopped at the other day. A blue jay perched on the roof tilted his head and squawked an obnoxious welcome. Could that horrendous building be the trading post?

She took another look around. It might be safer if she went to the building she recognized as Williamson's home. She could ask there for directions.

Sarah tossed a frightful glance toward the trees. Captain and Bessie's residence was at the far end of that stretch. She longed to hurry back to them, afraid the cost of independence was more than she was willing to pay.

She braced herself. *No, I cannot let Sammy grow up on others' benevolence. That is what I must keep in mind.*

An ear-splitting whistle penetrated Sarah's awareness. More

17

militia practice, no doubt. Did they think that noise would deter the warriors? Sarah could tell them from firsthand experience that that wouldn't work.

She took a deep breath. *I am here to find work, to turn my life around, to help Sammy. I have to reach these goals, no matter what I run up against.*

⋙

The man who peered at Sarah over the top of heavy spectacles seemed close to her own age of twenty-five. A sparse beard sprouted from his boyish cheeks, and freckles blotched his otherwise pale skin.

Sarah summoned a friendly smile. "Good day, sir. I just arrived and am looking for a list of work folks around here may need help with."

The young man's glance took in the worn hem of her gray, full-length dress before he gazed back at her. "Jeremiah said you-all was coming. Have a hard time on the trail?"

"I do not know any Jeremiah," Sarah replied. "But to answer your question, we did not run into any heathens."

"That does make the journey more tolerable. Oh, my! If my mama were here she would hang her head, 'cause I overlooked my manners. Rufus Putter, ma'am. Everyone calls me Rufe, or Putt."

"Pleased to make your acquaintance, Mr. Putter. Now about that list. . .where can I find one?"

"I hate to disappoint a fine-looking lady like you, but I cannot help you."

Sarah refused to give in to the urge to just plop down in the dust and cry. Other than sponging off the Halls, she had nowhere to go. She mustered her courage, knowing this was something that must be done in order to build a new life.

"I am fairly well trained in teaching and housekeeping," she offered.

"Most folks 'round here do not believe in schooling. As for housekeeping, none have enough to pay someone—"

"Rufe?"

The voice that intruded into their conversation was so commanding, Sarah's gaze snapped to the other side of the room. The soldier walking toward them nodded briefly at Sarah.

"Sorry for interrupting, miss," the newcomer said, "but militia business comes first." He turned back to the clerk. "I cannot find that last message from Major Whelp. Do you have any idea where it might be?"

The men debated the issue while Sarah tried not to listen. She told herself it didn't matter, but the boldness in the newcomer's voice would fill one of the Allegheny valleys she'd recently traveled through.

As the clerk and the new arrival walked toward the rear of the room, Sarah followed, studying the room with a wary eye. A crooked table held a few books and an inkwell and quill. The few pieces of furniture appeared to be on the verge of collapse.

Sarah returned her gaze to the soldier with the vibrant voice. He was tall and apparently in charge. Then *he* was the person she should talk to about work.

"Go look," the soldier directed the clerk. With Rufe gone, he leaned against a table, crossed his arms in front of his chest, and gazed at Sarah.

Sarah knew what he saw. Her hem was muddied and torn, her hair tangled from a run-in with a low-hanging branch, and her shoes almost worn through the sides. Though he stared at her, Sarah didn't think he meant to be rude. He seemed to be focusing on her eyes. They gazed at each other until the clerk cleared his throat.

"Sir?" Rufe prodded.

"What?" the soldier snapped. "Is this a lassie of yours and you need to finish making plans to meet with her later?"

The idea that she could be anyone's lassie made Sarah want to giggle. She took a good look at the soldier again. His hair was beyond midnight and full of soft curls that whirled over his brow. She had a sudden urge to push them back away from his eyes, much as she might her son's tousled mop.

"I am not his lassie," she said, finding it difficult to quit looking at him.

If his hair was beyond midnight, his eyes reminded Sarah of a morning mist, with a smidgen of mischief in their depths.

He looked between her and Rufe and chuckled. "You do not know what a relief it is to hear that, miss. If you were, it would not say much for your character. But seeing that you deny knowing this scalawag we call Rufe, you must be a good sort."

Sarah sensed that the soldier was joking. Still, his praise warmed her from head to toe, and she drew in a deep breath to stay focused.

"Since you appear to be in charge, perhaps you can help me," she said. "You see, I just arrived with the Halls, and Bessie. . .er, Mrs. Hall, sent me to the trading post to see if anyone might have need of help. I am very adept with children. I can also teach, if there is need."

"Did you memorize that or just make it up on the spur of the moment?" he teased, slanting the clerk an amused glance.

"I assure you I am well qualified in these areas," Sarah replied briskly.

He held up his hands in surrender. "I do not doubt that. I am surprised to see you here, that is all."

Sarah frowned. "You make it sound as if few women ever come here."

"From what you said earlier, it sounds as if you are in search of the trading post," he said. "This is David Williamson's home—or, rather, this end is his office. We mostly see volunteers for the militia in here. Have you come to volunteer?" The twinkle in his eyes accented his grin.

Sarah's face warmed. "Oh! You think that I thought this is the trading post. Well, I did not see a sign to indicate that building. I thought someone here would point me in the right direction."

His smile aimed right for Sarah's lonely heart. "So you are looking for what we laughingly call the 'post with the most'?"

Sarah didn't want to stammer, so she simply nodded.

"I will escort you there," he offered. "I have been in Washington County awhile. I have not lost a young woman yet who has been directly in my care."

"What about your militia business?" Sarah managed.

"You would be doing me a favor," he assured her. "I am tired of studying plans that make no sense. Not to mention trying to decipher correspondence that seems written in a foreign language."

Relief flowed through Sarah. It wasn't her. He wanted a break from his demanding workload.

"I will take her, boss. You can get started on your reply to Major Whelp," Rufe said, holding out the misplaced message.

"No. Since the colonel left me in command, I feel it is only proper that I escort the lady."

Sarah wasn't sure about being alone with this soldier; his presence seemed to swamp her soul. Her good intentions wavered. It would be nice to have someone as brawny as he at her side. Perhaps it would curtail the rude comments some made when they saw her alone.

He settled a wide-brimmed hat on his head and motioned for her to precede him. Sarah swept in front of him, reminding herself that at the very least she must thank him for his help.

❧

Outside the building, Jeremiah drew her to a halt.

"Before we go any farther, I feel duty bound to introduce myself. County Lieutenant Jeremiah Stewart at your service. My duties include providing protection to pioneers who search for freedom and land in this area, along with a few other choice things which I am not at liberty to discuss."

"That is quite impressive, sir. I am Sarah Troy. . .er, Lyons."

"Troyer-Lyons," he repeated. "Is that one or two words?"

"One." Oh, dear! That wasn't the truth. She had not used her maiden name of Troyer in years. Why did it slip so naturally to her lips now?

"Mighty pleased to meet you. It is miss, correct?"

"Miss is only appropriate for those who have not wed," Sarah answered. "That is not true of me."

Her reply curtailed any hope Jeremiah might have about getting to know her better. Which was a good thing, he reminded himself. With the colonel off on a family matter and Major Whelp out in the field, he was in charge. He didn't have time for lollygagging around with women as Rufe liked to do.

"So you are married then." Jeremiah motioned for Sarah to step along. "Just my luck. I meet a beautiful woman, and she is unavailable."

"Oh, but I am not. . ." Sarah fell silent as a blush crossed her cheeks.

"Available or married?" Jeremiah scolded himself the moment the words were out. He must forget the way his heart leapt when he looked into Sarah's eyes. Only one woman had made him feel so. . .alive.

"Married," Sarah replied. "Not anymore." A hint of memory slowed her words.

"I am sorry," Jeremiah responded. "I did not mean to bring up something that appears to pain you greatly."

Sarah fussed with her dress sleeves, giving Jeremiah a

chance to study her. Hair the shade of ripe summer grain dangled down her back in some sort of fancy braid. High cheekbones accented exquisite brown eyes that Jeremiah found it easy to lose himself in.

Forget it, Stewart. No one will ever take Jenny's place.

Sarah raised her chin, insecurity glittering in her eyes. "Thank you for. . .your concern. Losing my husband is something I am still getting used to. I do have a son, though, and that is why I am here. To search for a way to provide for him."

"I admire you for that." Jeremiah watched her eyebrows rise at his compliment.

Sarah cleared her throat. "I made a mistake earlier," she said. "Troyer was a slip of the tongue. It was my name before I wed." Her gaze moved to the pasture, where several horses grazed.

Jeremiah reminded himself that he didn't have time for this sort of folly. As a matter of fact, he should have insisted Rufe escort her to the store. He had too many things to do and not enough time to do them in, before the colonel returned.

"Well, Mrs. Lyons, let me officially welcome you to our humble village. I hope you find what you are looking for. It is not often we get a lady like you here."

"Mr. Stewart," Sarah began with perfect diction, "I am here because the Captain and Mrs. Hall talked me into coming along. With my son, of course."

"Captain and. . .why that means. . . How old is your son?"

"A few months beyond four, but Sammy was well behaved on the trip. I am rather pleased for Bessie, I mean Mrs. Hall. . . . Being with child, well, she needs all the rest she can get."

"Mrs. Hall is with child?" Jeremiah gasped. The next time he saw Bessie, he would wring her neck. After she presented him with a niece or nephew, of course.

Sarah wrinkled her forehead. "Do you know her?"

"Yes. Quite well."

"Captain said they had family in the area."

"They do," he affirmed, mentally making plans to visit his sister. He'd been out yesterday when they arrived. Upon his return, Rufe had thrust a mess of paperwork at him, insisting that Jeremiah take care of it before he did anything else. By the time he finished, it was well into the night.

"I was only recently promoted to the rank of county lieutenant," Jeremiah said as they began their walk to the post. "I hope that is not disappointing to you."

"No. Why should it be?"

The confusion on Sarah's face told him she had no idea why he'd brought that up. Jeremiah didn't know either. He was fortunate she was so proper, for he was making eight kinds of a fool of himself. He would have to keep his distance, despite the attraction he felt for Sarah.

He motioned toward a tumble-down building. "Here is where you made your mistake. You should have gone past Colonel Williamson's home before you stopped."

"Someone should have erected a sign, but thank you." There was a small admonition in her voice, but Sarah's gaze lingered on Jeremiah's.

A group of soldiers exited the post and spilled out onto the path. Some had learned this morning that passes to see their families had been denied. They glared at Jeremiah and Sarah.

He realized that the men resented him. *So be it*, he told himself. *I might not like my current assignment, but if they don't get their training straight, this whole territory will disintegrate.*

"I will take care of erecting a sign immediately," Jeremiah promised, moving so as to shield Sarah from the glaring looks tossed her way.

"Watch your step." Jeremiah placed a hand on her elbow and guided her around some horses. "Things are rather difficult around here. I am not sure anyone will be able to hire you. What was it you hoped to do again?"

"Preferably something that allows me time with my son without causing trouble for my employer—if any such thing exists, that is."

Sarah didn't sound very hopeful. Jeremiah was sorry that he'd squelched her expectations.

"Allow me." He opened the door and waited for her to go ahead. "I did not mean to sound skeptical. Perhaps you will find someone who will be happy to give you work."

"You do not have to apologize. I am used to men who think women are unable to fend for themselves. Let me tell you something, Mr. Stewart. I have been the sole provider for my son for almost two years, and I will continue to do so. If that causes a problem, perhaps I should go back to. . .where I came from and not contaminate this piece of land."

Jeremiah didn't blame Sarah for sounding aggravated; he'd spoken before he'd thought. That was something he was going to have to work on. Suddenly he wanted more than ever to succeed, especially around Sarah Lyons.

four

Sarah trudged back to the cabin. While she watched Captain and Bessie unload the wagon, she gave her new home an impassive glance. The walls gave only a hint of solidity, the door hung crazily on its frame, and the chimney appeared as if it were tired of seeing the same sights every day. But with some fresh chinking, the cabin would keep the elements out, which was more than could be said of the house she'd left a few weeks ago.

Sarah watched as Bessie gave directions and Captain did his best to follow them. *That is what a family is supposed to be like,* she thought, ignoring the brutal twisting of her heart.

Sammy spied Sarah and threw himself against her. "Mama! You back."

Sarah hugged Sammy, knowing that he grew anxious when she was not with him all the time. "Yes, dear. I hope you were good for Miss Bessie while I was out."

Captain wiped a fine line of sweat from his forehead and joined Sarah and Sammy near the wagon. "Samuel is one fine boy. He did quite well carrying things into the house. He also picked out his room and said his mama would help him with it later."

"Thank you for watching him," Sarah said. "I do not know what I would do without you two."

Bessie joined her husband, leaning against a barrel of flour still tied to the wagon.

"Are you feeling better?" Sarah asked. When Sarah left earlier, Bessie was suffering from queasiness.

"I am now," Bessie answered. "I thought women only got ill in the beginning of their childbearing time."

"I guess we are all different," Sarah said.

"That we are," Captain affirmed. He drew Bessie against him and planted a noisy smack on his wife's cheek. "I am so glad this one is mine."

Bessie placed her hands on her hips and tossed him a mock frown. "Why do you say that, Daniel Hall?"

"Because you are good for a person's spirit." Captain sneaked another kiss.

Though Sarah saw them like this often, she marveled that two such opposites were man and wife. Daniel, known to most as Captain, was more apple-shaped than anything. The silver sifted through the brown at his temples made him appear twice Bessie's age. Bessie was generally outspoken and devoted her days to taking care of her husband. Sarah frowned. She and Levi had enjoyed the same sort of camaraderie displayed by the Halls until—

"Did you find the post, dear?" Bessie's query disconnected the chain of thoughts that might have sent Sarah into tears.

Sarah held Sammy close. "I ended up going to the Williamsons'. A very nice militiaman showed me the correct place to go, though."

"A very nice militiaman? What did he look like?" The peskiness in Bessie's tone could only mean trouble.

"You know I do not pay attention to those things." Sarah waved off the question, yet the memory of Jeremiah's misty eyes hovered in her mind.

"You ought to," Bessie said frankly. "A woman should not be alone these days, what with the war and all. Besides, our Lord made woman so man would have a companion. Right, Captain?"

He nodded, about all a man *could* do when Bessie got started.

"I appreciate your concern," Sarah said, "but I have been alone for so long, it seems like it has never been any other way."

Not long enough to forget, though, Sarah's heart reminded her.

"You are never alone," Bessie contributed. "Whether you believe it or not, the Lord steps right along with you everywhere you go."

"You know I have not seen much evidence that God is anywhere near me lately," Sarah replied. "Now please, can we leave it at that?"

"Yes, of course. Did you find work?"

Sarah shook her head. If she spoke, she might regret what she said.

"I was so sure you would," Bessie said. "I guess the war changed more than just the men who fight it."

Sarah gave an inward groan. She understood why Bessie chattered on about some things, but the war? Sarah knew it had something to do with the colonists wanting their freedom from England. At sixteen, she joined a group that fled Pennsylvania, in 1772, to settle in eastern Ohio. Nine years had passed since that time.

Does Callie still live in that Christian settlement? Fear stirred in Sarah's stomach. She'd promised Levi that she would take Sammy to find their relatives. What if she finally got there and they weren't there?

No! I have to believe I will find them. This move is a step toward that end.

"You know we counted on you staying with us," Bessie interjected. "We have four rooms. Besides, I think Captain likes your singing voice more than mine."

Sarah silently agreed. Bessie's best effort sounded like a wounded screech owl falling out of a tree. "I just do not want us to be a burden."

"We enjoy having you and Samuel with us," Captain inserted.

"We would not have asked if we did not," Bessie agreed. "Perhaps we will help you past that sorrow that haunts your eyes. We will pray for you. That will help."

Bessie grabbed a handful of tablecloths and moved toward the house. Captain followed behind.

Sarah gazed around at the open trunks and quilt-wrapped dishes representing Captain and Bessie's marriage.

I don't envy Bessie because she has a husband and a child on the way, Sarah admonished herself. *I don't.*

❧

"You could at least have written and told me I was going to be an uncle," Jeremiah said as he released Bessie from an almost rib-shattering hug. He leaned down and offered to shake hands with the small boy who ducked behind Bessie's skirts. The child jerked back, sending a stack of kettles clanging to the floor.

Bessie patted Samuel's head, then squatted to pick up the items. "Captain believed the Lord called us to travel when we did. If you had known about it, you would have insisted we wait until after the baby's birth."

"You know me too well, little sister. Now, tell me how things are going in your life."

"I will admit that times are rough, but seeing you makes our trip worthwhile, Jer. Though Captain was certain we would be fine, I feared we would not make it here safely."

"Well, you did, so let us not think about what could have happened." Jeremiah motioned toward Bessie's growing midsection. "You look good. Marriage to Captain agrees with you?"

"It does." Bessie clasped Jeremiah's arm. "I need to thank you for the support you gave me when—"

Jeremiah pressed a finger over her lips for a moment. "It was not me who pulled you through, it was the Lord. You know that."

"True," Bessie confirmed. "Now it is your turn, Jer. If you will allow Him, God will send the right woman to heal *your* heart."

Jeremiah cleared his throat. "Let us get one thing straight, Bessie Josephina. The condition of my heart is not available for discussion."

"I will drop it. For now," Bessie added with an impish tone. "By the way, Captain checked for you when we got in. No one seemed to know where you were."

"Out rounding up more men for the colonel's militia. I am glad you made it here safely. Makes my day a whole lot lighter."

"Those we care about generally do that," Bessie responded. "Where is your house, by the way? Is it close enough for me to walk to?"

Jeremiah told her he lived two valleys and a creek away. The first owners had tired of worrying about whether or not the Indians would choose them as their next victims.

"It is not a home, though, if you know what I mean," he finished.

"They never are unless there is love in it," Bessie advised. "How is Pa? You heard from him lately?"

"Got a letter last week, only he did not write it," Jeremiah replied. "A woman named Hazel signed it. She said they got hitched a few months ago and we were—"

"Pa got tied again?" Bessie interrupted. "But he said he would never marry again."

Jeremiah had nothing to say. Other than losing Jenny, their mother's death was the most horrifying experience of his life.

Jeremiah decided to steer the conversation to a safer area.

"Who is this little fellow who keeps hiding behind your skirt?"

Bessie moved aside and smiled down at Samuel. "This is my brother, Jeremiah. Can you say hello to him, Samuel?"

Samuel laid his head against her leg and refused to speak.

"Be patient with him, Jer," Bessie explained. "Strangers make him nervous."

"But who is he? You did not just pick up a small boy and cart him off."

"I would love to have a house full of children like Samuel. He belongs to Sarah, the woman we brought with us." Bessie gazed around the trading post. "Now where did she get off to? I wanted you to meet her."

Jeremiah raised his eyebrows. "Sarah?"

"Yes, Sarah Lyons. It is a long story, Jer. She lost her husband almost two years ago. She was living with some friends of ours. Captain and I could not see leaving her on her own any longer. We are determined to help her put it all behind her, but I do not know. Sometimes Sarah seems stuck with memories that I fear she may not ever be free of."

"Indians?"

Bessie nodded. "Sarah will not yet talk about it."

"I understand."

"I knew you would, big brother. You lost the apple of your eye. Speaking of Jenny, you cannot let what happened to her ruin the rest of your life. After all, I put Martin behind me."

"Jenny did not destroy me," Jeremiah insisted. "Yours is a different story. Besides, it seems to me you have enough to worry about with that little one on the way that you should not be fussing over me. Have you forgotten I am older than you and that I can take care of myself?"

Bessie wagged a finger in the air. "If that is true, when did you last sit down to a home-cooked meal?"

"I do not get those often," Jeremiah admitted. He wouldn't

have traded his memories of growing up with Bessie for anything, but sometimes Jeremiah wondered why the Lord put them in the same family. Bessie would have been better off with seven sisters so they could cackle over new quilt patterns.

Bessie grinned. "Mmm-hmm. That is what I thought. And that is exactly why you must eat with us tonight." She swished her skirts. "So there, Jeremiah Stewart."

"I have work to do, Bessie—you know that. Wait. You do not know, do you?"

"Know what?"

Jeremiah told her about David Williamson's election as commander. "You remember that I mentioned in my letters that he sometimes does crazy things?"

"So?"

"Believe me, Bess, I feel awkward about this, and I do not like it one bit."

"Tell me what it is." Her voice grew in pitch.

"Are you sure?" Jeremiah couldn't help dragging out the suspense as he'd done in their childhood.

"As sure as I am that if God does not hold this against you on your judgment day, I will. Let me hear it."

"Well," he drawled, "if you insist."

Bessie stomped a foot. "Now, Jer!"

He chuckled at her aggravation. "Williamson came up with this notion to make me a county lieutenant."

Bessie was never this quiet.

"Did you hear me?"

Bessie glanced around. "But you are. . .how in God's great world did he pick *you?*" Despite her disbelief, pride shone in her eyes. "How could he do that? I mean, you are not even. . .I thought all you did was deliver messages."

Jeremiah hooked his thumbs into the pockets on his jacket.

"Williamson does anything he sets his mind to. I believe, dear sister, his exact words were, 'This is my county and I will. . .' oh, never mind. Suffice it to say that the colonel can do pretty much whatever he wants."

"Then you are definitely coming to eat with us tonight. Anyone with such high rank must be properly fed in order to work at his best. I will be able to brag to your nieces and nephews someday that I fed their uncle, the next commander of the Washington County Militia. Supper is at six o'clock. My house."

"I will not be the next commander," Jeremiah began. "I only have a few months left, and—"

His words fell on deaf ears. Bessie was waltzing away, her hand wrapped around little Samuel's. Jeremiah wasn't upset with Bessie. She always acted this way when she considered a conversation finished.

As he watched them walk away, his heart ached for the youngster at Bessie's side. Perhaps he should have made more of an effort to get the child to say something? No, if Bessie had thought that necessary, she would have seen to it. She always knew when to push and when to leave things alone. Jeremiah admired that in his sister.

Perhaps it wasn't so bad having Bessie for a sister after all. She just might put a few pounds on his slender frame!

❧

"Is the pie ready yet, Sarah?" Bessie dashed around the tiny area she considered the "eating room."

"Yes. I tossed a dash of sugar on top before I took it out. It looks as good as it smells."

Sarah finished placing plates, utensils, and tea-filled mugs on the table. She was glad it was almost time to eat, for Bessie had been a bundle of nerves all day. Sarah didn't know what her part in the evening was to be. Since she was indebted to the Halls for giving her and Samuel a place to stay, she would do her best to not embarrass them.

"Could you get the door?" Bessie called. "Our company has arrived. I am not able to leave the stove."

"On my way," Sarah assured her, smoothing the front of the dark blue dress Bessie had foisted on her.

Sarah fixed a welcoming smile on her face and swung open the door. The man who'd been so kind as to show her to the trading post filled the door frame.

"You? What are *you* doing here?" Sarah spouted.

Jeremiah swept his hat off and bowed. "Good evening, Mrs. Lyons. Of course it is me. Whom did you expect?"

"Bessie. . .er, Mrs. Hall, did not tell me who was coming," Sarah admitted.

Jeremiah chuckled. "That sounds like my sister."

"You are Bessie's brother?" Land sakes, she found it hard to concentrate when those gray eyes of Jeremiah's stared at her.

"For the last twenty-three years," he confirmed.

"But she never mentioned. . ." Sarah peered around him. "Where is your wife? Will she be along later? She is not ill, is she?"

Jeremiah gave a short chuckle. "I take it Bessie has not told you much about me."

"Such as?"

"I am not married." Jeremiah's tone was suddenly sharp, as if he didn't want to talk about it.

That was fine with Sarah. The subject of marriage didn't appeal to her, either. *I have no ties to anyone.* The words echoed in Sarah's mind.

"I am sorry," Sarah murmured, wondering why the fact that he had no mate seemed to stick in her mind.

"Sorry I am not married?" Jeremiah stepped in, pausing to

scrape his boots across a rug. "I have nothing against those who choose to wed. It is just that I have decided that marriage is not for me."

Bessie's entrance saved Sarah from having to comment.

five

Jeremiah hugged Bessie and murmured a greeting. "You get prettier each time I see you, sis," he remarked.

Bessie laughed. "That is because there is more of me, Jeremiah. I am so glad you finally get to meet Sarah." Bessie gazed between the two of them.

Jeremiah gave Sarah a friendly smile. "Actually, I met Mrs. Lyons the other day when she searched for the trading post."

"A nice young militiaman," Bessie muttered, her eyes moving between Sarah and Jeremiah.

Jeremiah studied Bessie. "Why did you not tell her I was your brother?"

Bessie shrugged. "I suppose there were too many things going on, with the move and all. I have to sit down; my feet are killing me." She plodded away.

Jeremiah shook his head. *Bessie is about to play matchmaker again, and if I'm not wrong, the pretty young widow is oblivious to Bessie's scheme.*

As Jeremiah trailed after Bessie, he reminded himself that he wasn't looking for commitments. His memories of Jenny served quite well to fill his lonely hours.

"Jer? Would you mind. . ." Bessie glanced over his shoulder. "Where is Sarah?"

"She scooted down the hall as soon as you came in here, Bess. If I did not know better, I would say she does not want to be around me."

Bessie finished stirring a pan of gravy and tapped the wooden spoon on the side of the pan. "Nonsense, Jer. Sarah needs to be around people like you. That is exactly why we brought her here. Someone has to help her get over those appalling memories she carries."

"If you do not keep your voice down, she will hear you," Jeremiah cautioned.

"Perhaps that would be best."

Jeremiah spun a fork in a circle. "There are some things you cannot force people to forget, Bess."

"And as you well know, there are some people you cannot force into doing what is right for them."

"Well, that settles that." Jeremiah grinned. "You cannot fool me, Bessie. That look in your eyes says you think we can help each other get over our grief."

"I would never encourage two people to get to know each other if they are not good for each other," Bessie stated.

Jeremiah feigned surprise. "Let me guess. You think Mrs. Lyons and I would make a handsome couple."

Bessie shook the utensil in her hand at him. "What is wrong with that? You think there will never be a woman to take Jenny's place. You are right, Jer, but you cannot spend your life looking for a copy of the woman you loved. You have to accept the one that the Lord sends. Even I know that."

"I do not believe there is anyone out there who could take Jenny's place, Bess. But should Mrs. Lyons ever feel the need to divulge her troubles, my shoulders are broad enough to take whatever she wants to share."

"Captain said much the same thing. So far Sarah has not shared much about what happened to her, so I cannot say what she will think of your offer. It does make *me* feel better, though."

Good thing it helped his sister, because Jeremiah didn't like the way Sarah had already woven herself into his thoughts. If he didn't watch it, he'd be first in line to do as Bessie asked, to help Sarah get beyond her pain. He might not like it, but he was a soldier, at least for another few months. He didn't have time for a woman, especially one that did not seem impressed with him.

❧

Bessie put aside Sarah's concern about joining them for the evening meal by saying, "Samuel did not take a nap today. He will be fine playing all by himself. I took a plate back to him and he seems quite happy. Quit worrying about him."

Sarah thanked Captain for holding her chair and listened as he offered the blessing. She added a silent plea of her own that she would not say something humiliating. The aroma of steaming beef and buttered potatoes soon filled the small room.

Sarah listened to the others converse about the growing tensions. She wished she'd paid more attention before when Bessie spoke about the war.

How was I to know I would end up sitting next to a soldier? I don't want to impress him anyway, she fumed to herself.

The evening meal passed with laughter and smiles passing between Bessie and Jeremiah. It was obvious that they'd grown up in a house full of love and that both had missed seeing each other over the last few years.

Captain finished eating and pushed his plate aside. "I believe I have forgotten to congratulate you on your promotion, Jeremiah."

Jeremiah sighed. "I will be honest. I do not like what Colonel Williamson did one bit."

"He must have had a good reason to choose you," Captain said. "I cannot imagine he would put just *anyone* in such a delicate position."

"He said he needed someone the men could trust, that I was one of the few who could read and write. Still. . ."

"But that speaks highly of you, Jeremiah. From what I have heard, Williamson's word is law in these parts, so there is no chance anyone will rebut what he has done."

"Only Major Whelp, who is gone right now."

"It does not sound as if you can change the way things are," Captain said. "If you do not feel comfortable with the task given you, I trust you are praying?"

"Daily," Jeremiah commented. "I am committed to staying until the end of December. I know I cannot walk away from the job because that would leave everything in an uproar. Besides, there are several messages recently that have come in about the Praying Indians. Someone has to deal with them."

Sarah's spoon clattered to the floor. She dove toward it before Jeremiah could assist, but she felt his eyes follow her every move as she recovered it.

Captain went on as if he hadn't noticed. "Sometimes the demands of the job are discomforting, especially when we feel unprepared to handle them. I imagine there is someone who is helping you learn the way things are done."

Jeremiah nodded. "Rufe Putter, the colonel's clerk. We have become close friends since we started working together."

"Ah, yes. Rufe. I met him shortly after we got here," Captain said. "He seems to be a wise, though sometimes immature, fellow. As far as the militia is concerned, I am sure he knows things that you do not."

"He seems to," Jeremiah concurred.

"Sounds to me as if you are afraid of responsibility," Sarah blurted out. She munched on the inside of her cheek. *Will anyone notice if I climb under the table?*

Jeremiah's mouth curved in a small smile. "Perhaps wary would be a better choice of words, Mrs. Lyons. There are so many things to keep straight, I am worried that I might forget something important."

"Call her Sarah, Jer. That other sounds so stuffy."

Sarah jerked her glance across the table, where Bessie primped one side of her upswept hair, oblivious to Sarah's discomfort.

"May I?"

Sarah snapped her head toward Jeremiah. "Sarah will be fine," she said tersely.

"Then you must call me Jeremiah."

"I will," she agreed. There were few with whom she was close enough to use their first names. The thought of such familiarity settled within Sarah like lead.

Jeremiah's gaze held hers. "I believe Sarah was Abraham's wife's name."

"Good point, Jeremiah," Captain said. "I admire the Old Testament Sarah's patience while she waited for the Lord to bless her."

"Amen to that," Bessie seconded. "It is my opinion that the Lord provides exactly what we need when we need it. We only need to accept what He sends."

"What do you think, Sarah?"

Jeremiah sounded sincere, but he gazed at her as if she'd sprouted carrot tops behind her ears. Sarah patted her hair. All seemed well, but why were her fingers shaking?

"Yes, that Sarah was a rare woman," the present-day Sarah concurred. She regretted that she did not recall much about Abraham's wife. It had been so long since she had actively studied God's Word that much of what she knew had withered away. Her heart flinched uncomfortably.

Over the next few hours Sarah listened as Bessie and Jeremiah shared more stories from their childhood. She refilled coffee mugs and sat quietly until Captain exhorted Jeremiah to tell what he could of events in Washington County. When Jeremiah spoke of a few incidents and politely skimmed over the barbarity involved, Sarah's soul experienced anew the devastation associated with the Indian attacks. She chewed on her bottom lip to keep from saying anything.

"Some say the Praying Indians in Ohio are the ones we must keep an eye on," Jeremiah finished.

"But they. . . What makes you think it is them?" Sarah knew she should not have spoken so forcefully, but she couldn't help it. She knew some of those people. They were Christians. How could anyone suspect them of murderous deeds?

"There are several reasons that I cannot discuss right now," Jeremiah responded.

Sarah kept her voice even. "I refuse to believe that those Praying Indians are responsible for attacking innocent white families."

"Why do you say that?" Jeremiah challenged.

"Because. . .well, I just do," Sarah said. "Do not ask me to explain." She grabbed her plate and fled to the washroom.

A few moments later Bessie joined Sarah by the wash basin. She laid a friendly hand on Sarah's shoulder. "Are you all right? You look peaked. Let me do this."

Sarah shoved food scraps from the dinner plate into a bucket. "I will be fine, Bessie. It is you who should be resting. You have been humming with activity all day long."

"I understand," Bessie said. "I will leave you alone."

"How could you understand," Sarah murmured to Bessie's departing back, "when not even I do sometimes?"

❧

For the next few days no one spoke of Sarah's outburst, which made her feel worse. She and Sammy played together, went on walks, and searched for shapes in the clouds. No matter where she went, there was always another family to remind Sarah of her personal situation.

Sarah desperately wished God had taken their home and

spared her husband. She was thankful she and Sammy had not perished, but. . .why had Levi been killed?

Sarah pushed the depressing thoughts away. If she continued to think about her loss, she would end up in tears. She found her mind returning to the night Jeremiah visited.

There was no excuse for her outburst at Jeremiah. He was a visitor, and Bessie's brother, not to mention someone whose job it was to protect the settlers. Sarah was in Washington County to make things better for her son. Jeremiah did not mean any harm when he had discussed the Praying Indians. He was just passing on information. But he was a member of the militia. If the militia suspected the Praying Indians of the attacks, Sarah must be careful to avoid appearing too concerned about them. If people thought she sympathized with a band of redskins, who knew what would happen to her plans to build a new life for Sammy?

❧

Jeremiah watched Sarah and her son as they walked along the riverbank. Though it had been a week since he'd last seen Sarah, his heart stirred at the sight of her.

It is not fair to Jenny's memory, Jeremiah warned. His heart didn't listen. While he watched Samuel tossing handfuls of leaves on Sarah's head, Jeremiah let his heart dream. . .of a day when he might stand with Sarah and laugh with her as Samuel played. Of a time when he might be able to—

"Mr. Stewart?"

The closeness of Sarah's voice jerked Jeremiah out of his reverie.

"Good day, Sarah," he said, striving to sound unaffected by her presence. "Are you enjoying our beautiful fall weather?"

"Yes," she replied. "We went by the trading post but there are still no jobs available. I thought I would bring Sammy out to get some fresh air."

"I know how demanding a move can be. Are you getting settled?"

Sarah patted her son's head. "We are. And Sammy has not had any trouble sleeping as I feared he would."

"By the way, I thought we agreed last week that you would call me Jeremiah."

"So we did." Sarah leaned down and adjusted Samuel's sleeves, apparently wanting time to think.

"I am glad you did not have trouble on the trail on the way here," Jeremiah commented. "There are so many dangers out there, and running into warriors would tend to make a trip quite troublesome."

Sarah's shoulders stiffened. Compassion for her washed over Jeremiah. *No,* he warned his heart sternly. *Keep your distance.*

Sarah rose and studied him. "It has been my experience that some heathens are good people. Or are you one of those who blame all of them for the actions of a few?"

"I do not blame an entire tribe for something a few renegades do," Jeremiah responded. "If you knew half of what I do, you would realize that there are several tribes who will use any excuse they can to attack whites who may or may not have done anything to them."

"Has anyone ever asked them why they go after helpless families?"

"Usually there is no time to ask that question," Jeremiah replied. "They are too intent on retribution for what the British have convinced them is unfair treatment by us pioneers."

"Well, I suppose as a militiaman you must do your duty, regardless of the facts."

Jeremiah cringed. He should tell Sarah that his being a militiaman was not by choice. He was stuck in this job for another three months, whether he liked it or not.

"Look," Jeremiah began, as nonthreateningly as he could. "I promise that while you are here, I will do my best to not let harm come to you or your son."

Sarah's eyes widened. She took a step backward. "No one can keep a promise like that."

"My primary obligation is to ensure the safety of those who live in our community," Jeremiah assured her. "That means I will do my best regardless of who those individuals might be or what happened to them in the past."

Sarah hugged Samuel close to her side. "I know what you are trying to say. I do not need a man, Mr. . . .Jeremiah. Men only complicate matters and cause undue heartache. Regardless of what your sister seems to think, I did not come here to find a man."

"I am simply trying to make you feel welcome," he said.

"I can appreciate your concern," Sarah replied. "But I suggest that any further contact we have be limited to discussing the weather. Agreed?"

Jeremiah wished he could do as Sarah asked. He had thought long and hard about her comments at his sister's home last week. He figured Sarah must know more about the Praying Indians than she wanted others to know. If she did, and he could learn what it was, it might help their militia efforts in some fashion.

"I cannot do that, Sarah," Jeremiah replied. "There is something you and I must discuss that most definitely does not involve the weather."

six

Jeremiah strolled toward the office in Williamson's home, his earlier conversation with Sarah replaying in his mind. Instead of gaining her trust so she would talk more openly to him, he had pushed her away.

Perhaps that is best, he mused, stopping for a moment. A web of soft sounds borne on the wings of a bitter wind surrounded him. The only voice was that of a sentry whose duty was to shout the alarm should warriors appear.

Jeremiah felt comforted knowing the man he had chosen to watch through the hours of darkness was one of the best in the county. His heels plunked on the wooden floor of the part of Williamson's cabin that was devoted to militia business. He headed to the corner that contained a table, a wobbly chair, maps tacked onto one wall, and a very tall stack of reports.

Jeremiah took a deep breath. He must put aside thoughts of Sarah Lyons for the moment and prepare his mind for what lay ahead. In eighty-three days he would be released from the militia. Jeremiah recalled how, in April, the colonel had gathered the men around him and announced that Jeremiah was their new lieutenant.

Jeremiah secretly had hoped the men would rebel. If they had done so, he thought that would have convinced Williamson to change his mind. Instead, they had cheered their approval.

Jeremiah pushed out a heavy sigh. All right, then. He didn't like it, but God obviously intended to work another lesson in his life. He'd do his best at this job until his term ended.

People—including his sister and Sarah Lyons—counted on him for their safety. He was duty bound to protect them. Not that Sarah Lyons needed any protection. She seemed quite capable of verbally handling anything that came her way.

Jeremiah groaned. Sarah popped into his mind more every day, which wasn't fair to Jenny. Jenny was the woman he had loved. Jenny was the woman who should fill his days. Jenny was. . .gone.

Let her go. Learn to look ahead.

Though he'd had those thoughts before Sarah came along, the words had echoed louder in Jeremiah's heart each day since he met the young widow.

"The past," Jeremiah mused out loud. "If not for the past, Sarah would not be here."

As if that statement had cleared his mind, he opened the journal on the table. Jeremiah leaned back in the chair, propped the book on his knees, and flipped to the opening scrawl.

❧

A few weeks later Sarah was still without work. She took it upon herself to do most of the household tasks as a way to repay the Halls for their kindness.

Shooing Sammy back from the table's edge, she rolled a steaming loaf of bread from the pan. The crusty end was Sammy's favorite treat, and he eagerly awaited it.

"Smells good, Mama," Sammy complimented in his best begging tone.

Sarah handed him the end piece and watched as he happily scampered away. At least Sammy would have a warm place to live this winter. She wondered what would have happened to them had they not moved to Washington County.

"I am so glad Captain remembered to stock the wood pile before he left last week," Bessie said, garnering Sarah's attention. "Seems like it gets colder each passing day."

"Captain does seem to remember to take care of every little detail before he leaves on his circuit rides," Sarah said. "You are fortunate to have such a caring mate." She offered Bessie a slice of bread.

Bessie patted her stomach. "I think I had better pass on that. There does not seem to be much room in here for anything but the baby lately."

They sat quietly as Sarah finished chewing her bread.

Finally Bessie broke the silence. "Do you mind if I ask a nosy question?" At Sarah's shake of the head, Bessie went on. "I just wondered if you happen to know something about those Praying Indians the men were discussing last month?"

Sarah swallowed hard. "I suppose you could say that."

"You know, it might be of some help to Jeremiah if you told him what you know," Bessie said.

"Well, Mr. Stewart will not get any useful information from me," Sarah declared. "What I know is hardly worth the trouble of asking about."

"But it might help the militia," Bessie answered.

Sarah stood up. "I did not come here to help the militia," she stated.

"If you know something, then I do not understand what you will not tell him," Bessie persisted.

Sarah drew a deep breath. "I just cannot do it, Bessie."

Bessie dropped the subject. Sarah reflected on why she didn't want to reveal her knowledge. For one thing, she refused to believe that the tribe she once worshiped with would kill a person. She knew the missionary who led them, recalled the hymns and other parts of the morning and evening worship services.

Those Indians would not kill anyone, regardless of their skin color, Sarah thought. *They journeyed to Ohio to gain religious freedom, to avoid battling white folks who wanted to pen them into a tiny area hardly big enough to support a family, let alone a whole tribe.*

Should she attempt to prevent them from being blamed for something she did not believe they could do? What could she say that would make a difference?

The solution flashed quickly to mind. She could tell Jeremiah what little she knew. No, she realized, she couldn't. If she disclosed what she knew about the tribe, Jeremiah would discover her secret. Sarah frowned. There didn't seem to be a way to convince him without revealing her past.

ঽ৯

Though his heart wasn't in it, Jeremiah smiled at the woman at his side. The colonel's niece, Gemma Winslow, was staying with the Williamsons while her parents built a new home a few counties to the west.

Gemma had a cute pixie face surrounded by a halo of reddish-gold curls, but she was too short for his liking. As Jeremiah listened to her chatter, he added to his mental tally that Gemma also was simply too talkative. He forced himself to pay attention.

"So," Gemma said, "I said to Uncle Davy that he simply must allow the men more time to see their families. Do you not agree that is a grand idea, Jeremiah?"

"Actually—"

Gemma's beguiling look cut him off. "The way I see it, the men need to know that their loved ones support them in their venture to serve their country."

"Well, I suppose you could—"

"Uncle Davy agreed to look into my idea as soon as he can. Ah, to be married to a marvelous-looking man who fears nothing and is willing to give his life to defend this land from those dreadful heathens who insist on perpetuating those horrid atrocities." Gemma paused for a breath.

Jeremiah jumped up from his seat. "Please pass my thanks on to your aunt for the superb meal. I must go, though. Militia business calls."

Gemma frowned. "But you have been here hardly a half a hand of time, Jeremiah. Surely there is someone else who could do whatever it is that you do."

"Afraid not. I really must go, Gemma. It has been a pleasure talking with you."

Gemma stood and walked to his side. "You are coming back tomorrow night, are you not? I heard Uncle Davy ask you to stop by."

Jeremiah sighed. "Yes, I will be back. To discuss militia matters," he added, just to set Gemma straight.

৯

Sarah seated herself on the floor near the fireplace. Though the spot was overly warm, it did not chase away the cold in her soul. Sammy was abed for the night, and she planned on taking a few moments to relax.

Her thoughts circled from her childhood in an orphanage, to living with the Praying Indians, then to Jeremiah.

Why did he intrude so much in her mind? Why didn't he just join the ranks of other men she had met since losing Levi, men who had wanted nothing to do with her once they learned of her horrible past?

"I am just a lonely widow trying to set my life back to rights," Sarah said aloud. "If Jeremiah wants to know about the Praying Indians, he can ride there and find out for himself."

"He has probably already been through there when he was a courier," Bessie said. "If the issue bothers you so much, Sarah, why do you not tell him so yourself?"

Sarah realized Bessie had heard what she said. Though nervousness gripped her, she crossed the room to a chair. "I just might do that, Bessie."

"Good," Bessie said, harrumphing as she plopped into her own chair. "You do that. I know he wants to see you again."

"You cannot fool me, Bessie Hall," Sarah said. "You are playing matchmaker again, just as you did with Mary Logan and Tom Pittman. I do not like it, and I would appreciate it if you stopped."

"Mary and Tom are happily married," Bessie replied. "And despite what you think, there are decent men in this world. Matter of fact, Jeremiah is one of the best men I know."

Sarah folded her arms in front of her. "I appreciate all you and Captain do for Sammy and me, but I do not think I need to remind you that I am not looking for a mate."

"You do not, but I have to admit something. . . ." Bessie grinned.

Sarah threw her hands up in the air. This wasn't going at all like she had planned. Instead, it was as if she stood in a cabin in the middle of the Ohio wilderness with her sister, who was spouting thou-shalts and thou-shalt-nots at her. A wave of turmoil rose within Sarah. If she'd listened to Callie, she wouldn't be in the situation she was in now.

"Say it, Bessie. You will not stop until you do."

"Jeremiah is not just any man," Bessie announced.

"I do not care if he penned the Declaration of Independence," Sarah replied. "I am not interested."

"He has been hurt before—a woman named Jenny. . . . That is all I am going to say." Bessie grumbled as she got up heavily and marched to the fireplace where she poked at some embers.

"It does not matter to me that he has been hurt," Sarah called out. "Everyone has at one time or another."

"At least you realize that much," Bessie commented. "Do you also know that most find a way to pick themselves up and carry on? Prayer helps, and so do friends."

"Besides you and Captain, I do not need friends," Sarah insisted. "I am quite capable of making it alone."

"What about God?"

"Sometimes I do not see a need for Him either," Sarah said. "If He was a loving God as the Bible claims, He would not have disrupted my life."

"He *is* a loving God, Sarah. It is only that you chose to look at what He gave you as trouble, instead of as a test to make you stronger." Bessie clucked her tongue. "The book of Matthew says, 'Come unto me, all ye that labor and are heavy laden, and I will give you rest.' What a divine promise that is." She gave Sarah a tender glance. "You say you do not need God and you do not need friends. In that case, I pray our heavenly Father has an easy life planned for you."

"This is beginning to get old," Sarah warned. *"I* am in control of my life, no one else."

"That is where you are mistaken," Bessie replied. "God always has everything to do with your life. You just have to learn to trust Him again."

Sarah jumped from the chair. "How can I trust Him when I know what He took from Sammy? I may sit and listen, Bessie, but that is why I do not participate in Captain's Bible studies. I find it hard to believe in Someone who allows such cruel things to happen."

Did I truly mean that? Sarah was so flustered, she didn't know. Nothing seemed to work the way she wanted; perhaps nothing ever would. Going it on her own couldn't be any worse than walking with God, could it? Two years ago God let her down one too many times. Everything since that night only proved her need to stand alone. Why couldn't Bessie see that?

"That is exactly why I believe in Him, Sarah," Bessie said. "I have no doubt that He is always with me." Bessie patted the child within her. "Yes, God sometimes takes away that which we love the most, but if we are patient, He will send us other blessings. Not to make up for the ones we lost, but to show us that we are His children and that He loves us."

Sarah shook her head. "You cannot tell me you are content to sit around and wait for God to work a miracle."

"Captain is a miracle, as far as I am concerned," Bessie said. "Someday, when you are ready to listen, I will tell you what happened to me. And I am convinced that no matter what tribulations God allows me to endure here, He will make up for my difficulties in the Great Beyond."

"You are the most stubborn person I have ever met," Sarah replied.

"Guess that is why I survive what life throws at me," Bessie said. "Jeremiah is the same way."

"He does not look as if he has survived that woman you mentioned," Sarah commented.

"So you did notice him." Bessie grinned like a cat who just caught the last available mouse.

Alarm tightened Sarah's throat. "You do not have to raise your voice, Bessie. What I noticed is that Jeremiah appears uncomfortable around me," she explained.

"Why would a man who is not afraid of going out into the unknown to fight something he does not understand be uncomfortable around someone like you?"

"Why are you asking me? You should ask Jeremiah that question."

"I think you should ask yourself that, Sarah."

seven

"This man wants the job, Lieutenant Stewart."

Jeremiah pushed aside the journal to scan the candidate for courier who stood beside Rufe. Tall and rangy, he was just shy of being gaunt. Black hair spilled over his ears, and his features seemed fixed in a perpetual sneer.

With Colonel Williamson out again, Jeremiah had no choice but to acquaint himself with the only applicant. He introduced himself.

"Just call me Shade," the newcomer stated.

"Has Rufe explained the responsibilities of the job?" Jeremiah asked, thinking that the man's name certainly matched his solemn features.

"Yes." The man kept his dark gaze locked with Jeremiah's.

Jeremiah felt uneasy, but he continued. "You do not have any questions?"

Shade shook his head.

"Why are you so willing to work with us?"

Shade shifted his weight to one hip. "Call it evening the odds."

There was an air of edginess about Shade. *Just what I need,* Jeremiah thought. *Someone who is out for revenge.* "You do not talk much, do you?"

"No need to talk. Action is better."

"We do not pay much," Jeremiah offered, intrigued by the confident air Shade possessed.

"Don't need much."

Jeremiah didn't have much choice. The colonel had

announced the job to the men, but none had stepped forward to accept it. "Well, then, I reckon you will have to do," he told the man.

"Reckon I will," Shade answered.

Jeremiah narrowed his brow. Rufe had done the preliminary work; all Jeremiah must do now was confirm the selection. He recalled Captain telling him to trust the clerk's judgment. Jeremiah would do that, but a prayer that this wouldn't be a decision that would haunt him couldn't hurt.

The interview over, the new courier gave a two-fingered salute to his brow and eased out the door with the elegance of a mountain lion. Rufe followed him.

Jeremiah's gaze returned to the journal. He'd have to finish it later. There was another matter he had to take care of first, one that had developed over the last few days, no matter how hard he tried to ignore it.

"Rufe, I am headed to the trading post. Got a few things to take care of."

❧

Sarah dashed into the house. She almost tripped over Sammy, who played with his blocks in the middle of the floor. After assuring herself that her son was fine, she shouted for Bessie.

"Miz Bessie upside down," Sammy contributed. He made a *V* with his fingers to show his mother what he meant.

Oh, dear! Had Bessie fallen? Sarah's heart bobbled to a halt. *What should I do?*

She realized she must find Bessie and see what had happened. Sometimes the woman poked her nose into places where it didn't belong, but Sarah didn't want anything to happen to her. She shouted Bessie's name again.

Bessie's reply came from the back room. Sarah rushed down the hall. She found Bessie leaning over and holding her ankles, exactly as Sammy had shown with his hand motions.

"What are you doing? You are over seven months along. You could hurt yourself." Sarah bent down to peer at Bessie's flushed face. "Have you no sense?"

"I only wanted to see my toes before they disappeared," Bessie explained. "I did this last week and did not have a bit of trouble getting back up. But now look at me!"

Sarah had done the same thing when she carried Sammy. Levi had joked with her and told her that if she'd been any shorter or further along, she'd have been stuck in that position. Sarah was glad Bessie wasn't huge, otherwise she could imagine that very thing happening to her.

"You do not hurt anywhere, do you?" Sarah perused the V-shaped woman.

"No. I just cannot seem to get the motion going to stand back up. Will you help me?"

Sarah moved in front of Bessie, grabbed both arms, and tugged gently upward, ready to counterbalance if need be. When Bessie stood upright, her eyes shone like lanterns on a winter night.

Bessie fanned herself. "How embarrassing. Please do not tell Captain. He would skin me alive if he knew I did that."

"I did something similar once," Sarah confided in a burst of intimacy. "I will not tell if you promise not to do it again."

"You do not think I hurt my child, do you?" Bessie looked stricken.

"I do not know, but it did not seem to injure Sammy."

"Oh! I promised I would watch him for you. I plumb forgot. Did you see him?"

Sarah explained that he was playing by the door. "How long were you like that, anyway?" Now that her initial agitation had faded, she relaxed a little.

"Not long. Honest." Bessie collapsed onto the edge of her mattress. "Whew. That was refreshing. You sound out of breath. Why were you hurrying so?"

"Well, I went to the trading post, and you know I was not really expecting anything, but there it was."

"What?" Bessie sounded suspicious.

Sarah was too excited to care. "A notice that someone wanted a laundress."

"Who?"

"It didn't say."

"You mean you do not know who you will be working for?"

Sarah frowned. "No." Not knowing hadn't seemed important until Bessie pointed it out. "The clerk at the post just said I could pick up and return the work there."

"And he gave no hint as to who it was for?"

Sarah paced the small room, chewing on her lip. "No. Do you think I should refuse since I do not know who I will work for?"

"Oh, no. I did not mean that," Bessie gushed. "I am sure whoever it is has a reason for keeping their identity hidden."

Sarah caught her hands behind her. "It does sound strange, but this will allow me to contribute to the running of your household. You know how guilty I feel about accepting food and lodging from you."

"We have all known hard times. It is only proper that we help others when they need it. Captain and I would not have asked you to come with us if we did not want to share." Bessie pushed off the bed. "I think we should celebrate your hiring with a cup of tea."

"Only if you promise to sit, like a woman with child should," Sarah admonished.

"Yes, ma'am." Bessie giggled as she ambled down the hallway. "I cannot believe I could not get back up. Oh, Sarah. What would I have done if you had not come back just then?"

"I do not know." Bessie's gratitude tugged at Sarah's heart.

She didn't need commitments like that.

☙

Jeremiah closed his eyes and rubbed the bridge of his nose.

Lord, you know what is in the next entry as well as I do. I'm scared, Lord—afraid of what I will do when I see the words. Be with me, Lord. Help me through this.

He opened his eyes and focused on the date: August 14, 1779. He knew he must read this, if for no other reason than to put it behind him. He blinked to clear the blurry words he was about to read.

"A band of Wyandots were shot not far from here by a Fort Pitt detachment. We are positive that the heathens were responsible for the recent deaths of Jenny Townsend and her brother."

Sorrow wedged in Jeremiah's throat. He dropped the journal, not caring that it landed on the toe of his boot. Jenny Townsend—his promised, his beloved. Tears burned his eyes. Jenny, with her carefree laugh, her long, dark hair, and her way of making everyone she talked to feel more loved, more precious.

Pain dug through Jeremiah's heart. He didn't push it away. It was time he faced his loss. He could have avoided reading this and not recalled the horror of Jenny's death, but hadn't he done that for too long? Hadn't he lived within himself, not reaching out to others as he should?

Yes, he had. That wasn't how his parents had raised him.

"Blessed is the man that maketh the Lord his trust." Jeremiah's mother had quoted that verse from chapter forty of the book of Psalms at the table every morning. Later Jenny had adopted the practice herself. If nothing else, Jenny Townsend had believed in Jesus.

That's what I must remember, Jeremiah consoled himself. *Jenny may not be here with me, but she is in heaven with our*

Lord, and with my mother.

Jeremiah repeated the statement until it seemed branded on his heart. With a deep sigh, he drew the book back onto his lap and hardened his heart as he reopened it.

Once past the heartache of the first entry, Jeremiah tried to make sense of other writings, which detailed the successes and failures of pioneer families. Being unable to concentrate, he slid the book out of sight and formed a triangle with his pointer fingers and thumbs.

Why did You put me here, God? What is it I have yet to learn before I move on?

He thought back on his childhood. He'd grown up content to help his parents eke out a living until he was old enough to learn the blacksmith trade. Though he barely made a success of that, he enjoyed working with animals. When the courier position arose shortly after his mother died, Jeremiah decided to apply for it.

"You are running off to war," his father had argued.

"No, Pa. I am going to help my country in its search for freedom."

"Believe what you want, son, but you will end up killing those who God put on this earth."

"I am just a courier, Pa. I will never kill," Jeremiah had promised.

In the end, after all the disagreeing, there was nothing left to say. As a courier, he thought he would not rise above the enlisted ranks. Now he was a county lieutenant, with the potential to control the fate of an entire county.

Perhaps I should write Pa, fill him in on all that's happened. Or perhaps I should wait until after the birth of Bessie's child?

Jeremiah's gaze settled on the candle on the desk. He followed wisps of smoke rising from it as they traveled toward the ceiling's gloom. It wouldn't hurt if he posted a letter to his father tomorrow. He would tell him about Bessie and the young'un on the way, about Captain and how he appeared to have helped Jeremiah's baby sister get over her grief. He might even mention Sarah Lyons, if for no other reason than to let his father know she'd suffered as great a tragedy as Jeremiah himself. The only thing he wouldn't tell his father was what he was doing in the militia—no use upsetting Pa any more than necessary.

❧

Sarah scrubbed shirts until she thought her arms would fall off. Even though the position offered her scarcely enough to buy Sammy a hard candy every week, she wanted the clothing to be as perfect as possible so she wouldn't lose the job.

Bessie still thought Sarah should ask who'd hired her. Sarah was reluctant to do so. If she were successful at this, she might garner more work. That would provide her a way to raise Sammy, and that was what was important.

Bessie had taken Sammy to see Jeremiah, as she did daily. Before she left, she insisted that Sarah use her portion of soap, as well as the hot irons. Promising to reimburse Bessie for the lye soap, Sarah agreed. She had propped the irons against the grate to heat, and glanced over to check them. Satisfied that she wasn't going to get the shirts any cleaner, she wrung out the water and hung them near the hearth. Wiping her hands on her apron, she sauntered to the large room, where she straightened a few of Bessie's knickknacks.

Noticing that the quilt across the back of Captain's chair was skewed, Sarah moved to straighten it. One of Sammy's blocks lay in her path. She stumbled over it, her hand flinging out and knocking Captain's Bible off the chair arm. The book fell, its pages ruffling. A flash of yellow drifted downward like an autumn leaf.

Sarah glanced around until she spied a sliver of yellow ribbon tied around a lock of hair. Whose was it? It didn't matter whose, she had to put it back. But where? Her sister would have stashed a small object such as this in a specially marked place within God's Word. Sarah hadn't touched a Bible in years, let alone opened one.

It's just a book, she told herself. *Just because I've decided to go it alone doesn't mean anything will happen if I open it.*

Sarah studied the volume, knowing there was only one thing she could do. Finally, she picked up the book and raised the cover. Inside, a spidery inscription read: "Presented to Daniel Hall and his second wife, Bessie, on the occasion of their marriage. Given by Johanna Hall—December 25, 1778."

It took Sarah a minute to recall she'd heard Bessie call her husband Daniel occasionally. But it was the phrase "his second wife" that baffled Sarah. She had not suspected that Captain had been married before. Did Bessie know? Oh, what did it matter anyway? Whatever had gone before in Captain's life meant little to Sarah.

"Was it not Psalms that Captain declared his favorite?" Sarah murmured to herself.

Thinking she might lay the tuft of hair there until she found out for sure where it belonged, she slid a finger between some pages in the middle of the book and turned to the book of Psalms. As the rustling pages settled into place, verses sprang to her mind.

"He that dwelleth in the secret place of the Most High shall abide in the shadow of the LORD."

"I waited patiently for the LORD; and he inclined unto me, and heard my cry."

They were words that had given hope when there was little else to cling to. As a new Christian, Sarah once had believed their promises. Now she trusted only herself. Misery filled her heart.

Why did I make the choices I made? How can God ever forgive me for not trusting Him as I should have all this time?

Sarah stifled a sob. Instead of concentrating on the path she'd chosen, she needed to decide what to do about the snippet of hair. She couldn't go through the Bible page by page hunting for evidence of where it belonged, could she?

Why not? Captain was out for the day, and Bessie was gone visiting. Neither would return for a few hours. She had nothing else to do until the shirts dried.

It was just her and the Bible.

With trembling hands, Sarah turned to the beginning and searched for the familiar words. *"In the beginning God created. . ."*

The fingertips of her right hand lingered on the words. The small indentations where the letters pressed into the thin paper nestled against her skin as if they belonged there.

God's Word. This was what her sister, Captain, and Bessie, and so many others as well, put their trust in. Fragile words printed on delicate paper.

"The word of the Lord stands forever."

Sarah shook her head. "Now where did those words come from?"

The memory crept slowly to mind. It was from a sermon the Moravian missionary David Zeisberger had preached—on a fine fall day filled with laughter, sunshine, and friends—just after the group arrived at the site where they would build their wilderness mission.

"The Lord knows your sorrow, knows your pain, but He can only take your burden if you let Him."

Who was that? Levi's mother, who did not yet know her only son had passed on. Sarah brushed away the drops that slipped down her cheeks and splotched the tiny letters.

"Stop crying," she chided herself. "Tears don't solve anything. All they do is pull my heart into my throat and make me feel as if the whole world is collapsing around me."

Sarah pressed a thumb and forefinger between her eyes and took a deep breath. Feeling composed, she turned the pages one at a time, renewing her search for something that identified where the tiny remnant of hair belonged.

❧

Jeremiah listened as his sister argued with Rufe in the outer office. Shortly after her move to Washington County, Bessie began coming by daily. She claimed the exercise and fresh air were good for her health, but Jeremiah suspected she really wanted to check on him.

Jeremiah knew he should go out to greet Bessie, but Shade's latest delivery lay on the table, an unpleasant reminder of the newest task Jeremiah had been given.

"I am here to see Jeremiah." Bessie's loud announcement drew Jeremiah's thoughts back to the present.

"Lieutenant Stewart is busy, ma'am," Rufe replied. "He left orders not to be disturbed."

"But I am his sister. Surely he can see me."

Though Rufe was captivated by Bessie's outgoing personality, the clerk did as Jeremiah had ordered. "I am sorry, ma'am, but the lieutenant said—"

"I have some important business with my brother," Bessie interrupted. "I demand that you let me in."

Jeremiah envisioned Bessie leaning over the desk, her crazy curls falling around her shoulders and her bright eyes glaring at Rufe. It was almost enough to lighten his foul mood.

"I am sorry," Rufe began again, "but Lieutenant Stewart said no one was to interrupt him. In fact, Gemma was here earlier and he even refused to see her. Hey! You cannot go in there!"

"Jer?"

Jeremiah slowly raised his gaze. "Hello, Bess. And Samuel. How are you?" It was all he could do to keep his voice from breaking.

"Miah!" Samuel gave him a sprightly smile.

For the sake of the child, Jeremiah grinned back. "Hello, scout. Are you making sure my sister gets here safely?"

"I am," Samuel replied. He sauntered a few steps closer to Jeremiah.

"That is good," Jeremiah said. "I am glad you came with Bessie. Did your mama come along, too?"

Despite a constant hope that she would, Sarah rarely accompanied Bessie. If Sarah did, she went to the trading post while Bessie visited with Jeremiah.

"She wash shirts so she can buy me candy," Samuel explained.

"That is right," Jeremiah said without thinking.

"Jer? How did you. . . ," Bessie began. Understanding dawned in her eyes. "You?"

Jeremiah nodded, hoping the young boy did not follow their conversation.

"Why did you not tell—"

"I am glad you stopped by," Jeremiah interrupted. "Can I walk you home?"

He sent Bessie a silent plea with his eyes that said, Please don't ask me to explain why I didn't let Sarah know it was my laundry.

"Sure thing. Are you ready to go, Samuel?"

Samuel looked up. "Now?"

"Yes. Jeremiah is going to walk with us."

"He stay and eat with me?"

Before either Bessie or Jeremiah could answer, Samuel raced out the door. He sprinted ahead down the path, stopping to point out moss growing on the base of some trees and giggling at a squirrel scolding them from the branches overhead. Sunshine filled a cloudless sky, and as they walked, Bessie tucked her hand around Jeremiah's elbow.

"Go on, big brother. You might as well tell me what is bothering you."

"A spot of bad news, Bessie. That is all I can say."

"I have not seen you this upset since. . .I wish Captain were not out on his circuit. He would know what to say to you."

Jeremiah was sure Bessie had been about to refer to his behavior when he found out about their mother. It would be nice if Captain *were* here, but he wasn't. Jeremiah wanted the Whelp family to know what he'd learned before others from the community found out. The dismal burden pressed against his heart.

"I am sure Captain would be a big help," Jeremiah said, "but since he is not here, and neither is Colonel Williamson, this is something I must handle."

Jeremiah wasn't looking forward to taking the news of the major's death to his family. He hadn't liked the way Dan Whelp had pushed people around, but the man's earthly life was gone—snuffed out by a wayward arrow in the heat of conflict, for the little good that would do his widow.

Bessie studied him with a younger sister's patience. "It is about the war, is it not?"

"Look, Bess. I know you mean well, but—"

"If you promise you will pray, you do not have to walk us the rest of the way," she said.

I want to go with you, Jeremiah thought. *I want to see Sarah. And it will keep me from having to face Mrs. Whelp until I figure out what I'm going to say to her.*

"Seems as if I have been doing nothing but pray since I got this job," he admitted.

"Say no more." Bessie patted his arm.

Jeremiah wasn't quite ready to be alone. "How long do you reckon it is before your young'un is due?"

"Another couple of months. Why?"

"I thought I would write Pa. Perhaps he would like to know."

Bessie studied Jeremiah's face. "Pa is a survivor, Jer, just like us. He always told us we cannot stumble if we are on our knees."

Jeremiah nodded. There wasn't anything else to say.

eight

Bessie waited until Samuel hugged his mother and went off in search of his blocks. "Would you say all that again? I must have missed something."

Sarah repeated her story. "I tried to go back through a page at a time to find out where this tuft of hair went."

Bessie gave the item a quick glimpse. "It is not the Bible I am worried about, Sarah. It is you. You look different."

"What do you mean?"

"I do not know, but something about you has changed."

Sarah sought something else in the room to look at besides Bessie. She thought she knew what Bessie was referring to. As she'd leafed through the Bible, occasional passages had grabbed her attention, reminding her of the times when God's Word had soothed her troubled heart. Since she'd lost Levi, believing was so hard to do.

Sarah held up the lock of hair again. "I thought perhaps you could tell me where it belongs. I will return it to its rightful place, and I promise never again to pick up that Bible."

"That Bible belonged to Captain's grandmother," Bessie responded. "She carried it across the ocean when she settled here. Pick it up anytime you wish to. As a matter of fact, I would like you to do so. When Captain is gone, I do not get to hear the stories I love. You can read, Sarah. Would you?"

"Would I what?" Sarah asked cautiously.

"Read to me," Bessie said, caressing her abdomen. "I want my child raised in the Lord so he knows there is a reason for everything that happens in his life. This way he will get a head start."

Sarah's throat grew dry. "I do not think that is a good idea. I do not read very well."

"There is only one thing that is better than your reading, and that is your singing. It would mean so much to me. Please say yes." Bessie seldom begged, but she was doing it now.

When Sarah was with child, Levi had done everything he could to please her. Sarah didn't know why exactly, but making Bessie happy seemed important.

"Perhaps I could read a few verses a day," Sarah offered.

"You are so wonderful," Bessie squealed. "Captain will be over the moon. He has prayed for someone to study with me. I am so glad it will be you. Can we start right now?"

Sarah swallowed her discomfort. "I suppose now is as good a time as any, but what about this lock of hair? You still have not said where it goes."

"I think Captain keeps it in the book of Isaiah," Bessie said. "Just slip it in there somewhere. He will set it to rights when he gets home."

Sarah felt awkward just "slipping it in there somewhere," as Bessie suggested. Sarah recalled that one of her sister's favorite Bible chapters was Isaiah 40. She paged to it and tucked the hair away, silently reading a sentence there: *"They that wait on the LORD shall have wings like eagles; they shall walk and not become faint. . . ."*

"Wait on the Lord," Sarah repeated to herself. Doing so probably couldn't hurt. She'd waited for something to happen that would give her hope for the future since the day she had lost Levi. Perhaps there was something more meaningful that she needed to think about.

"Do you think you could start somewhere other than 'In the beginning'? I know it is important, but I am anxious to hear about Jonah, and Ruth, and Daniel."

Sarah drew a deep breath. Reading the words of the prophet Isaiah, she'd experienced a brief memory of comfort. She thumbed her way through the Bible so she wouldn't have to think about it. "How about Jonah first?" Sarah asked. "It is short and will not take us long."

And it describes exactly what I am feeling just now, Sarah realized, *as if I have been swallowed by an animal much larger than myself and have no means of defense.*

Bessie smiled. "I just love the part when Jonah finally realizes God is in control. How about you?"

꫞

Jeremiah entered the office, stamping his feet to rid his boots of the dust collected on his trip to Fort Pitt. He'd enjoyed the brief time on the trail, though he knew he wouldn't have gone if Dan Whelp were still here.

Jeremiah frowned as he scanned a note lying on the desk. Colonel Williamson had been in while Jeremiah was gone. He left an invitation for Jeremiah to meet with Gemma tomorrow night, with a postscript indicating that he was again gone to the farthest reaches of the county.

Sometimes I think the colonel only wants the glory of being the commander, not the hassles or heartache that go with it, Jeremiah thought. *No, that's not fair,* he corrected. *The colonel does what he can.*

Rufe cleared his throat and Jeremiah forced his mind back to the task at hand.

"What am I supposed to do with this mess?" Jeremiah pointed to a pile of papers on the desk.

Rufe shrugged. "You have done pretty well up to this point. Just tell me where to start, and I will get right to work helping you compose the answers."

Jeremiah studied the heaps. Five months as county lieutenant had done nothing to relieve his awkwardness at being a leader. He made decisions and wrote requisitions for supplies, but mostly he prayed.

"Want some time to look through them before you write the replies?"

"I suppose that will be best," Jeremiah said. "Especially since I might be tempted to quit if I wrote right now."

He stared at a hand-drawn map on the wall. Miniature red dots marked Indian attacks up and down the Ohio River and several points to the east. With each attack, the red circles marched closer to their settlement.

Jeremiah tried hard to follow two principles his father had taught him: Study a problem from all angles and figure out the best way to solve it. But he still doubted his ability to make the best decision. Perhaps all the trip to Fort Pitt had accomplished was point out that he missed hitting the trail and taking messages to leaders who would decide what to do next.

That's what it was. He'd never had this much responsibility before. He just carried others' decisions to those of higher rank. Perhaps that was part of his problem; he needed to take a step back and consider what it was he really wanted to do in life. That wasn't going to happen anytime soon. Not when the colonel refused to spend any time at home.

The next time Williamson returned, Jeremiah would insist Williamson select someone to fill Dan Whelp's position. Then Jeremiah would take a few days off, time he needed to clear his head. Perhaps he'd visit the grave he hadn't visited in so long. Then again, perhaps not.

You don't need to resurrect pain you've already buried, Stewart, he admonished himself.

Pain. At least a benefit to staying busy was that he had little time to think about Jenny. All the way to Fort Pitt and back he'd thought of. . .Sarah.

Sarah, who had the same hollow look in her eyes that echoed how Jeremiah felt when he thought of how wrong his life had gone since losing Jenny. Sarah, who appeared to feel that she was the only one who'd experienced great tragedy and would never find anyone else who understood.

Jeremiah understood, though he didn't like talking about it. Some things were better left alone. Scars healed faster that way, covering wounds that would otherwise always hurt if continually exposed. That's why he kept thinking of Sarah Lyons. Not because she was beautiful. Not because the sad look on her face dug furrows in Jeremiah's heart every time he saw her. Jeremiah buried his head in his hands.

Lord, what is it You would have me do? I do not understand why You have put me here, or what purpose I have in Sarah's life. And speaking of Sarah, do You think You might find a way to take away her hurt? When I see her standing off to the side where she thinks no one is watching, it's as if she sees something horrible run through her mind, over and over. Perhaps she does not know it shows, but it does. I trust You. Please help her, Lord.

Jeremiah opened his eyes to find the red circles on the map staring at him.

"Figure it out yet?" Rufe asked from behind him.

"Not yet, but I reckon that is why I do not sleep much. Gives me more time to ponder things."

"I will fire up the lanterns and stay with you," Rufe offered.

"What?" Jeremiah quizzed. "I thought you would probably go see that young lady you have been crowing about lately."

Rufe shook his head. "It did not work out. Seems the only one worth going after would be that pretty miss that wandered in here by accident a few months ago. But I got the feeling she wanted nothing to do with men."

"I think you are right, Rufe," Jeremiah said, ignoring how painful that understanding was.

≥⋆

Jeremiah glanced across the table. Gemma's cheeky stares were beginning to get on his nerves. He tried not to let his irritation show, but the more time he spent with her, the less he wanted to.

"You look so dashing tonight, Lieutenant Stewart," Gemma cooed. "I just adore the way that dark blue jacket brings out the gray in your eyes."

Jeremiah coughed. Mrs. Williamson glanced at Gemma but returned to sipping her soup without comment.

"Thank you, Miss Winslow." Jeremiah wished he'd gone to Bessie's instead of coming here. The colonel's request that he visit Mrs. Williamson and Gemma was not a military order, but Jeremiah felt bound to do as the colonel requested.

"Did you know," Gemma began, "that Uncle Davy has insisted that I spend the whole winter here? Now, is that not just the most wonderful news? I miss my parents, of course, but to stay here with aunt and uncle is an opportunity that I cannot put aside."

"How nice," Jeremiah murmured, though it really didn't matter. Once Gemma started talking, she didn't need encouragement from anyone. His sister sometimes chatted incessantly, but Bessie was family—he *enjoyed* listening to her. Gemma, on the other hand. . .

"And so," Gemma went on, "since my mother just absolutely has no skills where cooking and sewing are concerned, I plan to learn those sorts of housekeeping details from Auntie while I am here. Must be prepared to be a proper wife when the day arrives, you know." Gemma flashed him a coy smile.

Jeremiah lowered his gaze and grimaced. Gemma left little

doubt as to whom she expected to be a wife to.

❧

Sarah opened the door to Jeremiah's knock. Her surprised look told him that he was the last person she expected. Jeremiah didn't know how to relieve her distress, so he simply asked if he could enter. While Jeremiah took a seat at the table, Sarah rushed to find Bessie.

"Bessie is taking a nap," Sarah announced as she returned. "Is there something I can do for you?"

"Yes. I came to deliver an invitation. There is going to be a Winter Supper," he said. "For everyone in Washington County. The main purpose is to fellowship and to celebrate the birth of our Lord. Will you pass the word on to Bessie and Captain for me?"

"I take it I am not invited."

You certainly handled that well, Jeremiah chided himself.

"Of course you are invited, Sarah. I meant that since Bessie is not available right now, I wanted you to let her know about the gathering."

"I will tell her," Sarah said. "But you can count me out."

"You have something against getting together with others to celebrate the birth of our Lord?"

"No," Sarah replied.

"I think Samuel might enjoy seeing everyone," Jeremiah urged. "I hope you will reconsider. The supper is designed to encourage the men of the militia and give the ladies a chance to dress in their finery."

"Well, Mr. Stewart, you will have to do without my presence," Sarah said. "The less I have to do with militiamen, the better. After all, if your counterparts at Fort Henry had responded to my late husband's request for protection, I would not be here today."

This was not going at all the way Jeremiah had planned.

"Point taken, Mrs. Lyons. I will not let your comment pass without saying that our military companions down river operate under different rules than we do. Please don't assume that I or our force here would have done the same. May I also add in our defense that if people would quit settling so far from others, there would be less chance of renegades, Indians or otherwise, upsetting their worlds."

"We thought we were out of the way," Sarah retorted, her voice rising in pitch.

"In this day and time there is no place that is truly out of the way," Jeremiah replied. "It becomes doubly important that we all help and encourage one another when we get a chance."

"That might be," Sarah acknowledged, "but I do not see a need to get myself involved in others' lives right now. I will not attend the supper."

&

"Tell me a story, Mama," Sammy demanded, climbing onto her lap and disrupting her line of thought.

She did as he asked, but Sammy soon fell asleep in her arms. While he dozed, Sarah stared at the whorl of hair on the top of Sammy's head. She placed a soft kiss on his brow.

"No matter how I try, Sammy, I cannot change what happened to us. Your pa and I planned for our lives to be filled with love and laughter. And that would have come to pass if those horrid Indians had not attacked us. I miss your pa, Sammy. Sometimes I miss him so much I cannot imagine how I am to go on without him. At least I still have you. I hope I can find a way to help you grow to be a man your pa would be proud of."

nine

Jeremiah figured he'd be pressed into escorting Gemma to the supper, something he definitely did not want to do. He wondered if perhaps he might convince Rufe to escort the colonel's niece and decided that he would discuss that idea with Rufe later.

With the colonel back demanding an update, Jeremiah pointed to an area on the map a half-day's ride north. "The latest report came from a family by the name of Clayton. They took the wife and two girls."

Williamson indicated some other dots to the south. "What about these?"

Jeremiah shook his head. "I just do not know. They usually are not this scattered. When they attack, they hit one or two close together, then disappear."

Good thing there is less than a month of my commitment left, Jeremiah thought. *I cannot wait till the Winter Supper, for I'll be released shortly after.*

"You are in charge while I am out in the field," Williamson said. "You read all the reports. Give me your input as to what you think is happening, lieutenant."

Jeremiah thought for a moment before he spoke. "I think the group of Indians responsible for the raids is getting nervous. They do not know what is going to happen, since their alliance with the British is becoming more apparent."

Williamson folded his arms in front of his chest and rested them on his portly middle. "A good analysis. I would like to add that after this latest trip of mine, I firmly believe the

Wyandots are not the ones we need to worry about."

"Why not?"

Williamson glanced to the dots spiraling out along various creeks that fed into the Ohio River. "You read those journals Rufe's father loaned to us. If I am not mistaken, it seems he believes the Praying Indians are the prowlers."

Jeremiah studied the colonel. Feeble candlelight gave him a sallow appearance and drew attention to his somewhat rumpled shirt.

"Those Indians are Christians, colonel. I cannot believe that they are to blame. Besides, I think that Colonel Brodhead out of Fort Pitt stirs them up on purpose."

"Brodhead is just trying to defend his territory, Jeremiah," Williamson replied. "Did you read the last report he sent out?"

"Yes," Jeremiah growled. "All that bragging about how they took three hundred men and killed fifteen warriors, then dragged the old men, women, and children away. They murdered most of them before going back to Fort Pitt. What is the world coming to?"

"My mother would say, 'Nothing good,' " Williamson offered. "Sometimes we can only react to an action. We do not control our fates. We do what we are pressed into doing."

Jeremiah flexed the fingers on his right hand. "They killed forty warriors they said were drunk and highly dangerous. Those braves were probably scared and running away. Brodhead didn't have to pursue them. I wonder if he had proof that they were guilty."

"Brodhead is on our side, lieutenant. What is the matter with you?" The colonel pinned him with a hawklike gaze. "Getting cold feet?"

Jeremiah raked his fingers through his hair. "I believe that as Christians, Zeisberger and his flock will not kill. Nor will I." He sought to remind Williamson of his promise not to take part in any such thing.

"I think there is something more than Brodhead killing warriors bothering you."

"Rufe's father wrote everything he could in those journals." Jeremiah hoped to turn the conversation away from death and dying.

Williamson nodded. "So?"

"I think I will read them again and see what else I can find out about those Moravian missions. If that fails, I may just take a short trip to Fort Pitt to see what I can find out from them."

"It will not change my mind, but do what you think you need to. I think they are guilty. That is all I need to know." Williamson's words were filled with bitterness.

❧

Bessie waddled through the door with Samuel pushing her knees from behind as if she couldn't make it under her own power. She was not far from giving birth, and though it wore her out, she insisted on going out each day for a short walk. Sarah remembered that awkward time when her body felt like a fruit that stayed on the vine too long. But the end was worth it—holding your child and realizing that God's blessings often came in the form of babies. As if he knew the joy he brought her, Sammy launched himself into Sarah's arms.

"Missed you, Mama." He planted a smack on her cheek.

Sarah's heart spun in her chest. Sammy looked so much like his father that she wanted to cry. What if she couldn't keep Sammy safe long enough for him to grow up?

"I missed you, too, Sammy." Sarah smoothed his hair behind his ears. "Looks like we will have to cut your hair soon."

"No hair cut. I want hair like Miah." Sammy pouted.

Bessie chuckled. "Guess I ought to tell you so you know what Samuel means. You know those daily strolls we take?"

Sarah nodded. "I do not understand how you can continue to go out every day. I sat at home and did nothing but wait for the big day."

"Family means a lot to me, and so I go to visit Jeremiah. He has been rather gloomy lately, and I do so want him to cheer up. You know that Major Whelp is. . .gone. Well, actually, I guess his dying is only part of the story."

Bessie had the geese ready to head south again, prattling on about things that made no difference to what she had started talking about. Sarah snuggled Sammy on her lap and prepared to stretch her patience.

"I am sure you remember Captain telling us about Dan Whelp being killed," Bessie continued. "I heard he wasn't well liked, God rest his soul, but anyway, with Colonel Williamson back, Jeremiah is upset because now he does not see any way out of this militia business. He only did it as a favor for Williamson, and in the beginning Williamson told him it was only for six months and now he says longer. That has Jeremiah all worked up. I just hope he does not do something he will regret later."

Bessie rubbed her arms. "Where was I? Oh, yes. Jer sent off some letters without telling the colonel about them. He requested that they appoint a replacement for Major Whelp. They—I forget who 'they' is, but they did not answer yet. In protest, Jeremiah decided he will not cut his hair until he is out of the militia. Says he is not made to be a militiaman and does not know what God is trying to do with him. Sarah?"

"Go on. I am listening." Sammy squirmed as if he were tired of hearing Bessie go on and on like a crow with a piece of corn stuck in its beak. Sarah let him down, knowing he would toddle off to his blocks. She considered joining him.

Bessie smirked. "Have you seen him lately?"

"Colonel Williamson? I do not even know him."

"Jeremiah, you ninny. Who do you think I have been talking about? You have not been paying attention, have you?"

"Partially," Sarah admitted. "He should hear soon, I would think," she said, responding to a part of the chatter that she recalled.

"He hopes it will be soon. He says this has been the longest year of his life."

"From what I have seen, I think he has done an admirable job," Sarah said.

"Shall I tell him you said that?"

"Why would it matter to him?"

"Jeremiah would be thrilled to hear it, but I will not let him know if you do not want me to."

"Let him know what?" Sarah glanced at Sammy. He played with his blocks near her feet. The way he leaned against her legs made Sarah feel as if she could conquer the world. Then she remembered that night a few years ago when she had failed Levi, and she went back to thinking the world often conquered her.

Bessie sidled to the washtub and swished some clothing around in the soapy water. "That you care about him."

In her haste to stand up, Sarah practically bounced Sammy off her leg. She checked on him before she replied.

"Owls and loons, Bessie. Jeremiah and I have nothing in common. We want none of the same things from life, and neither of us wants an involvement with someone else. We simply are not interested in each other."

Bessie tsk-tsked. "Jeremiah does not share those sorts of details with just anyone."

Sarah shook her head. "Other than the fact that he is not interested in marriage, he did not share anything with me. I simply guessed that is how he feels."

"Well, it was a mighty fine guess, because you are right on the mark. And you know what that means. . . ." Bessie turned away and hummed a tune Sarah hadn't heard before.

Sarah reached for a small piece of composure. "What *does* it mean, Bessie?"

"It means what I have thought all along. You two are meant to be together."

Sarah threw her hands up in the air. "I give up."

"I do not." Bessie swung around with her hands clasped around her midsection. "But I think we will put any further discussion aside, because it appears this young'un is anxious to make his appearance."

&

"Shade dropped this off, lieutenant. Do you have time to read it before you go see your new niece?" Rufe handed the missive to Jeremiah.

Jeremiah wanted to see the tiny angel God had blessed Bessie and Captain with, but he knew when duty came before family. He unfolded the parchment and spread it out in front of him.

Eyes have seen the big man across the lake. He says he is behind missionaries' plan to bring the gospel to Indians, but he still thinks they are guilty of treason. Captive Indians now stay south of Delaware village, south of the big lake where they build homes to stay through the winter. Many want to leave but are forbidden to. It is rumored that some will attempt a return to Muskingum valley in the spring—they want to collect the harvest left behind when they were captured in August. Prepare for attack from those who return.

Jeremiah rubbed his forehead. *The big man across the lake*

must refer to none other than the British commander at Fort Detroit.

"What did it say, boss?" Rufe moved toward Jeremiah.

"Please do not call me that," Jeremiah snarled. "That title belongs to Williamson."

"Sorry." Rufe backed off. "Must be some powerful stuff in there to upset you so."

"There is, but no signature to tell me who it came from. Go find Colonel Williamson. Let him worry about it. I am off to see my niece."

And Sarah? his heart asked hopefully. *Of course not. She doesn't want anything to do with me.*

His heart gave a huge sob.

ten

Jeremiah pressed a package wrapped in brown paper into Sarah's hands before disappearing down the hall. Sarah thought it a gift for the baby and laid it on the table.

She checked on Sammy and then gave a hurried peek into Captain and Bessie's room. There she caught sight of Jeremiah holding the new baby. The miniature bundle lay snuggled in his arms while he spoke with Captain.

Sarah slipped back down the hall. As she began ironing, she recalled Levi's excitement the night Sammy arrived.

"We got us a boy, Sarah. May he grow to be strong and true. May God help us raise him correctly."

Sarah paused to think about Levi's words. No matter what disaster befell them, Levi always trusted God to bring them through. If God was so loving, why didn't He save Levi from being killed? Now Levi would not see Sammy grow up. It was up to her to make the decisions that would influence Sammy's upbringing.

Anxiety whirled through Sarah. She wasn't the first woman to be left to raise a family, but she often felt like it. Other women had lost their mates to the Revolution or to marauding Indians. Most of them lived near family who helped them through a difficult time. Without family near, Sarah bore her grief alone.

"I believe the first of December is a fine day for a birth. What do you think?"

Sarah gazed across the room to find Jeremiah settling into a chair.

"Yes, it is a fine day." Sarah noticed that Jeremiah appeared tired. She offered him tea, but he declined.

"Bessie and the baby are sleeping," Jeremiah said after a moment of observing Sarah while she pressed a shirt.

"New mothers need all the rest they can get." She flipped the shirt over to begin working on a sleeve.

"I have heard that many times," Jeremiah replied. "Do you agree it is grand that God brought Captain back in time to see the babe during her first few hours?"

"The timing does seem fortunate." The crease in the sleeve refused to line up correctly. Sarah frowned at it.

"Those garments do not have to be perfect, you know," Jeremiah stated. "A small crook in the sleeve will not hurt."

Sarah straightened the sleeve and settled the unwieldy iron on it. "I appreciate your comments, but I prefer them to be as flawless as I can get them. Since you seem to be in no hurry to leave, I take it there is nothing pressing, as far as slaughtering Indians goes, demanding your attention?"

Jeremiah laced his fingers together and laid them on the table. "You know what, Sarah? This may sound strange, but I really do not go about hunting down Indians to kill. When I began working with the militia, it was with the explicit understanding that I wanted nothing to do with killing."

Sarah arched her eyebrows. "Then why do you not just quit?"

"Because I promised David Williamson that I would stay until the end of December, and I will, even though there are times when I wish I did not have to."

"Do you know what you will do when you leave the militia?"

"I was a blacksmith before, so I imagine I will return to that trade. By the way, Sarah, did you give any more thought to going to the Winter Supper?"

"I thought I made my choice clear earlier," Sarah said.

"So you did, but a man can always hope. Perhaps you will not want to go with me anyway, after what I am about to tell you."

Sarah's throat tightened. "And that is?"

"I came today not only to see my new niece, but to check on how my shirts are faring."

Sarah gazed at the garment in front of her as if it were a snake. *"Your* shirts?"

"Yes. Bessie and I have discussed my decision not to tell you many times recently. She will be pleased that you finally know the truth."

"But. . .why did you hide it from me to begin with?"

"Bessie told me what little she knows about your history, Sarah. She said you were trying to build a life for yourself and your son. I wanted—"

"Bessie had no right to. . . ," Sarah began in a shaky voice.

Jeremiah appeared at Sarah's side and laid his hands on her shoulders. "Bessie worries about you. She is concerned that if she does not get you involved with people, you will destroy yourself, and your son."

Sarah took a step back. "I did not ask her to fret over me. For your information, Sammy and I are quite fine without anyone's help."

"People worry because they care," Jeremiah said softly. "Why is that so hard for you to accept?"

Sarah turned from Jeremiah's probing gaze. She wanted to share the reason with him. If she did, though, she sensed he would become another in a long line of those who didn't understand why she had once lived among Indians.

Jeremiah strode back to his seat and stretched his legs beneath it. Sarah wished she could join him, let her heart reach out to him. To do so would invite danger. She shuffled some drying pots and pans.

"I did not hide the fact those were my shirts from you on purpose," Jeremiah offered.

Sarah faced him. She hoped her confusion did not show too plainly. "Then why did you have me drop them off and pick them up at the trading post? The way you did it makes it seem like charity."

Jeremiah shook his head. "I guarantee it is not charity."

Sarah relaxed. "Good. For that is the last thing I will take from anyone."

If I stay here on the other side of the room, I'll be fine, Sarah told herself. *Of course, leaning against the butter churn isn't comfortable, but I will not move.*

Jeremiah propped his elbows on the table. "You needed a job. I provided one. If you do not want it, I will be glad to find someone else."

"No! I need. . .er, I will keep it. I just cannot bear to be beholden to folks any more than necessary." Sarah wished she didn't sound so anxious.

"It is just a job, Sarah," Jeremiah said. "I am not asking for a lifetime commitment. The Bible directs us to assist widows and young children. That is all I am doing."

Perhaps that is the problem, Sarah reflected. *Despite the fact that I want to be independent, something about Jeremiah makes me want to reconsider that issue.*

Levi's face drifted through her mind. Sarah missed him, not as drastically as she had in the fresh days of grief; the pain had softened since she met the Halls. . .and Jeremiah.

"I feel guilty about taking a job someone else might need more than I do," she said.

"I did my own laundry before you came. You did not take anyone's job."

Sarah wrinkled her forehead. *He did his own laundry? Well, of course. Living alone in the middle of who knew where, all men in the militia probably did so.*

"I feel better knowing that." Sarah warned herself to keep her feelings about Jeremiah to herself, no matter how difficult that was when he was around.

"Me, too. I already told you I am not interested in women. But can we at least be friends?"

Sarah's heart sputtered. Besides Bessie and Captain, it seemed like forever since anyone cared about her in a personal way. She and Levi lived far from civilization, and they'd had only themselves to depend on. A lot of good that had done them. Being alone was awfully lonely. She knew that much after being around Bessie and Captain the last few months.

"I am not sure about being friends with anyone," Sarah confided. "Once you trade your life history and tell others things you consider important, they push you into corners where you do not want to be."

"I would never push you," Jeremiah said. "You are the only one who can put yourself in a corner, Sarah."

ॐ

Jeremiah reminded himself that he had come here today to visit his sister and see his niece, not to spend time with Sarah. Yet, the offer of friendship had come so naturally from his mouth that he wondered why it had taken him so long to make it.

"Friendship is all I *can* offer," Jeremiah said, hoping Sarah didn't think he was asking too much.

"I suppose it is hard for someone who has always had people close to him to understand," Sarah said, "but I am not like normal people."

"You are as normal as you let yourself be," Jeremiah replied.

Sarah shifted her stance. "I was abandoned by my parents when I was very small, then raised in a Philadelphia orphanage." She spit the words out as if they might do irreparable damage.

"I knew others who grew up without parents," Jeremiah replied. "They did not let that stop them from living and having friends."

"I also lost that home when a flood swept it away."

"Where did you go then?" Jeremiah recalled that he had once told Bessie his shoulders were broad enough to take whatever Sarah might wish to share. He sat up a little straighter.

"The orphanage owner knew a missionary, and his flock willingly accepted me. When they headed west, I went with them." Her words trickled with sadness.

"A missionary?"

"Is there something wrong with men who instruct others in God's Word?"

"No." Jeremiah thought of the missive he had read before coming to see Bessie and the baby. It mentioned missionaries. How many missionaries were there in Ohio? Only the Moravians that he knew of.

"Then why do you sound as if you disapprove?"

"I did not expect you to say something about them."

"I knew it!" Sarah paled.

"Knew what?"

"You are just like all the rest."

"The rest who?"

"Men!" Sarah crossed her arms in front of her and stared at him.

"How can you say that? You do not even know me."

"I know you well enough to know that all you think you have to do is snap your fingers and people will die!"

"Sarah, I have already explained that is not something I am comfortable with," Jeremiah insisted.

"Then why did you not tell me from the start it was your laundry I was doing? Were you afraid I would refuse it if I knew it came from you?"

"That is not it at all." Jeremiah couldn't figure out why Sarah changed the subject from the militia back to the laundry.

"Do not move from behind that table or I will scream so loud everyone within the county will come running."

"You do not have to scream, Sarah. I will leave on my own." Jeremiah moved toward the door, careful to keep as much distance between them as he could.

"Do me a favor," Sarah directed as he reached the passage.

Jeremiah was relieved Sarah had not called him Mr. Stewart. And he was absolutely crazy to ask what the favor was. He should leave this woman alone, since that appeared to be what she really wanted.

"What, Sarah? Tell me."

"Concentrate on your profession and quit worrying about the little people who make no difference in your life."

"Do what?"

"You heard me. Forget about those of us who do not matter to you. We are really quite capable of surviving on our own."

Jeremiah thought Sarah looked too pale, but what could he do? She obviously did not want any assistance from him. He hardened his heart, since it was the only way he could see to deal with Sarah's demand. "I thought we just agreed to be friends?"

Sarah glared at him.

"All right, but no one survives alone very long, Sarah. However, if that is your wish, I will do my best to uphold it."

eleven

Jeremiah patted Sarah's neck with his hand. "Come on. Wake up, Sarah."

When Sarah mumbled, the feeling of helplessness that had overcome Jeremiah initially when Sarah collapsed began to fade.

"Please, Sarah." Jeremiah brushed a lock of hair off her brow.

"Jeremiah?"

"Yes. It is me."

"What happened?"

"Well, I guess the only way to say it is. . .you swooned."

Sarah pushed her way up to a sitting position. "I will have you know that I never swoon. I thank you for assisting me, Mr. Stewart, but I am fine."

Sarah sounded determined, but she was shaking. "Are you sure?"

"Of course I am." Sarah shrugged her shoulders and shook her hands in front of her. "See? I am fine."

"What is going on out there?" Bessie's piercing question traveled down the hall.

"Nothing to worry about, little sis," Jeremiah called out.

"If you do not leave soon, Bessie will be coming out here to find out what happened," Sarah said. "She should not be up, having given birth only yesterday."

"I just want to assure myself that you are all right before I go," Jeremiah insisted.

Sarah rubbed the sides of her head. "Will you quit arguing

with me? You are giving me a head pain."

Sarah did *seem* to be herself. When she had slumped to the floor, he hadn't moved fast enough to catch her. He had worried that Sarah might have seriously injured herself.

Jeremiah thought himself strong and capable, but the sight of Sarah lying on the floor had twisted through him with vicious force. Without thinking, he brushed his hand across her forehead again.

Sarah shoved his hand away. "Bessie told me once that you are persistent. I guess she is right, but I honestly do not need someone to fuss over me. I am capable of taking care of myself."

Sarah wished Jeremiah would leave, for his arm around her shoulder felt too comforting as he helped her to a chair.

"I only want to help you," Jeremiah replied. "I am sorry if you think that what I am doing is wrong."

"It is not," Sarah said. "I am just tired of telling people that I am the only one I can depend on."

Jeremiah searched her face. "As far as I am concerned, leaning on others signifies courage, and there is nothing wrong with doing so. No matter what, I know of only one ultimate source of peace. I need to pray, Sarah. Will you join me?"

Jeremiah stretched a hand toward her and closed his eyes. He began to offer a prayer of thanks that Sarah wasn't seriously injured. When he felt the tentative brush of Sarah's fingertips on his own, he thought his soul would never stop singing.

&

How could things go so wrong? Jeremiah thumped his fist against his thigh. He thought sure he'd argued his point successfully, but Colonel Williamson refused to appoint Harry Ray to replace Dan Whelp. It appeared Williamson was bent on making Jeremiah the replacement instead.

Jeremiah shuddered. He could not, no, *would* not, accept the position. He'd voiced the fact that he did not believe in killing to the colonel several times during the last year.

But that wasn't Jeremiah's problem right now. Shade was hanging his outer garments near the fireplace; he surely did not bear good news. Weariness was evident in Shade's face as he turned toward Jeremiah.

"Eyes are again on the Praying Indians," Shade said, rubbing his hands together for warmth.

"What now?" Jeremiah grumbled inwardly that Williamson always seemed gone when something of import happened.

Shade frowned. "British commander accuses Zeisberger of treason last summer because missionary in constant contact with colonials at Fort Pitt. Missionary says he is friendly to both British and colonials and that he only want to be left alone with his Christian converts. British commander agreed Zeisberger could do so, as long as they stayed in the Wyandot village near the Big Lake."

"What else?" After dealing with Shade for several months, Jeremiah knew there was always a reason for everything Shade said. Sometimes Jeremiah just had to wait until later to figure it out.

"So now they stay in old Wyandot homes and search for food. The British promised them supplies, but the Praying Indians turn it down."

Jeremiah leaned against the table. "Mighty brave of them, since they were not allowed to carry much with them in the fall."

Shade's face grew solemn. "They brave people."

"Do they realize how fragile their situation is? They have the British pulling at them from one side and half of their own clan squealing on them. Not to mention that most of our militia is convinced they are heathens."

"They know what life means, and they believe God provides."

Jeremiah understood the strength in that. "Is there anything else?"

"One moon ago Zeisberger met with British commander again. Outcome a surprise to all there."

"I am beginning to see that anything the British are involved in does not turn out the way we expect," Jeremiah said. "What is the rest?"

Shade shook his head back and forth as if to the beat of a war drum. "Wyandot leader full of lies. He told British the missionaries were his friends. Not so. Wyandot and British are dangerous. Will cause the Christian Indians to die. Soon."

Uneasiness stole through Jeremiah's heart. "How soon?"

"Shade's bones feel sorrow."

Jeremiah paced back and forth between a chair and the hearth. "What do you really think is going to happen?"

"Your militia will be involved," Shade said. "Stop them."

"They are not my. . . Oh, never mind." Jeremiah tossed his hands in the air. "How will the militia be involved?"

Shade sighed. "Danger will decrease your friends. The settlers will insist army protect them."

Jeremiah's soul hit the bottom of his feet. "You mean there will be more attacks?"

Shade grimaced. "More vicious ones."

"It has been quiet here lately. I hoped they were afraid of our weapons, or that the weather was too cold for them."

"Except Great Spirit, real warriors are not frightened of anything. They will come again."

"I do not know how you know that," Jeremiah countered, "but I will warn everyone in the county to be more watchful. Let's suppose our men, and we are well over one hundred now, do want to fight. How do I stop that many?"

"You are wise man," Shade said. "Find a way. Remember, the eyes of all miss nothing."

Jeremiah sighed. He would definitely have to sort this out later. "Who are 'the eyes of all'?"

"Some men see but miss the important things," Shade replied, donning his jacket.

"So?"

Shade kicked at his moccasins. Clumps of half-melted snow fell onto the warm hearth and spat like an angry cat. "Not all tribes happy with whites in Ohio wilderness. Not all whites happy they in Ohio wilderness."

"That does not make sense," Jeremiah stated. "What are you trying to tell me?"

"Be wary of what others ask you to do, for not all are on your side. I must go." Shade eased from the room.

Jeremiah rubbed his neck. He propped his chin in the palm of one hand and studied the lines in his other palm.

What if Shade is right? What if there are more deaths? What if I get caught up in an upsurge of hate and Colonel Williamson orders me to kill someone? Oh, Lord, don't desert me if such a thing comes to be!

❧

At least I still have Sammy, Sarah thought as she watched her son play at her feet. But the years before he grew up and said good-bye would pass quickly, then she would be all alone.

"Is everything all right, Sarah?"

Sarah looked up to see Bessie raise Elizabeth to her shoulder and pat the infant's back.

"I know this must be a bad time of year for you," Bessie added. "Is there anything I can do?"

"No. I was just thinking that perhaps my sorrow is not so bad this year. Why?"

"I know it cannot be easy." Bessie gazed at her newborn. "No matter what people say, often time is not enough to heal our wounds. Just the other day you read chapter fifty-eight in Isaiah to me. Do you remember what it said?"

"Not really," Sarah admitted.

"If I recall, it goes something like, 'Then shalt thou call, and the LORD shall answer; thou shalt cry, and he shall say, Here I am.' See, Sarah? You can call on our Lord any time for any reason. He is always there, willing to love, to share, to bring you peace."

"Bessie, I hope that someday I will return to God's flock, but after the way He destroyed my life, I am just not sure how far off that day may be."

"God loves you, Sarah. So do several others. You do not know how happy it would make me to learn that you are ready to come back to our Lord."

Sarah stared at the fireplace, contemplating Bessie's words. Bessie never seemed to let events depress her. How did she keep such confidence that life would work itself out for the best?

Bessie broke the quiet. "The other day I heard you tell Captain you wanted to start teaching Samuel his letters. Do you think you could teach me at the same time? I never saw a need before, but now I would like to know how to read so I may teach my daughter someday." Bessie beamed a grin at two-week-old Elizabeth.

"It is not something you learn overnight, Bessie."

"I do not expect it to come quickly. It would not be too big a bother, would it?"

Sarah shook her head. "I did not mean to make you think that." Teaching letters would be easier than reading Bible stories to Bessie. Every story Bessie chose seemed to spur Sarah's heart.

"If we need something special, Captain can fetch it for us tomorrow," Bessie said. "That way we can begin after our evening meal."

Captain's one circuit trip since the baby's birth had ended. Unless there was an emergency, he planned to stay home for the winter.

"When I was little, we used the smooth side of a split log and a charred stick to write the letters," Sarah replied.

"If it was good enough for you, then it is good enough for me," Bessie declared. Samuel came to stand beside her. She lowered Elizabeth so he could reach out and tickle the baby's chin.

Sarah watched her son babble something to the infant in an incoherent language. With every day that passed, she and Sammy got more entangled in Bessie's and Captain's lives. When Sarah joined them for the journey here, she'd not foreseen that happening.

She thought she'd find something that would allow her to support her son and herself. She hadn't imagined how barren Washington County would be.

What will I do if I can't find something to help me support Sammy? I cannot live off of the Halls' generosity forever.

". . .telling Samuel about the music there is going to be. May even be some small treats for the little ones, you know."

Bessie's chatter intruded on Sarah's thoughts. She snapped her head toward the woman.

"I wish you would change your mind about going," Bessie said. "It will be good for you and Samuel, and that way it will all work out."

"What will work out?" Sarah quizzed, sensing something in Bessie's voice that she wasn't sure she wanted to hear.

"The seating particulars," Bessie confided with a sly smile. "If you are not there, the whole evening will be a disaster."

"Quit being so emotional. No one will notice if I am not there."

"Those who are important will," Bessie replied.

Sarah gave a troubled sigh. "What does that mean?"

"It means we are to sit at the commander's table," Bessie responded. "You have to go. Otherwise, that silly Gemma Winslow will end up sitting by Jeremiah."

Sarah's throat tightened. Gemma Winslow? She'd heard the name before but hadn't known that the woman had designs on Jeremiah.

It did not matter. She couldn't sit with men who were determined to do away with those she once lived with, even if those men included Jeremiah.

Sarah feigned indifference. "I doubt one or two missing people will be a catastrophe," she said.

"I think it would be to Jeremiah. He does not like Gemma, you know, but she seems determined to get him to notice her."

"Gemma is quite free to sit with whomever she wishes," Sarah answered, keeping her voice even.

"Well," Bessie went on, a sly smile curving her lips. "Everyone knows you are staying with us. It will look strange if you are not there."

Gemma Winslow's name rolled around in Sarah's mind. What did Gemma mean to Jeremiah? Was he seeing her? Courting her? Sarah found thinking on this to be painful.

"Have they chosen a replacement for that major who got killed yet?"

"No news from that quarter," Bessie replied. "Jeremiah does know he has another ninety days to serve. The colonel talked him into it."

"You must be mistaken. The last time Jeremiah talked about it, he said he wanted out of the militia so he can go on with his life."

"Oh, Jer does not want to do it," Bessie agreed. "He told me that he prayed long and hard before accepting. He decided that God must want something special of him if he keeps putting him in uniform. It would sure make Jeremiah's night if you went."

Something nagged at Sarah. A few weeks ago she consented to be Jeremiah's friend. She hadn't been too friendly since that day. To be fair, the times Jeremiah had seen her, he had not tried to push her into anything more than casual conversation.

And don't forget, Sarah's heart reminded, *Bessie linked Gemma Winslow's name with Jeremiah's.*

"I might go, but I refuse to borrow another of your dresses," Sarah muttered.

Bessie grinned. "Jeremiah brought me a package the day Elizabeth was born. I have not opened it yet, but I think we need to take a look."

"I thought he brought it for the baby," Sarah said, recalling him handing her the parcel.

"No. If Samuel will go fetch it from the corner near my bed, we can decide what to do."

While Sammy rushed down the hall, Sarah took a seat.

"The only reason I would even be interested in going would be to see what sorts of food the women bring," Sarah said.

"We will see," Bessie replied, a mischievous glow dancing in her eyes.

≈

"Are you sure I did not miss Shade when I ran home?"

"No, sir. He has not been here," Rufe assured. "Shade is always smack on time, too. Wonder what could be keepin' him?"

"I do, too." Though Jeremiah had resigned himself to another three months in the militia, he didn't like it. After much prayer, God had impressed upon his heart that the militia was where He needed Jeremiah to be for the time being.

In his courier days, Jeremiah had feared being strung up alongside a forgotten trail. Had that happened to Shade? A damp chill climbed Jeremiah's spine. No! He had to believe Shade would appear.

Jeremiah ambled to the door and peered down the wagon trail. He mouthed a verse from the fourth chapter of Philippians: "Be careful for nothing; but in every thing by prayer and supplication with thanksgiving let your requests be made known unto God."

He took a deep breath. Worrying did no good. He must trust God to take care of Shade.

Rufe began dousing candle wicks. "I am sure Shade will be here soon. Perhaps we can get him to stay for the big doings?"

"I will ask," Jeremiah said. "You know he is uncomfortable around people. He only stays long enough to deliver messages."

Jeremiah studied Rufe from across the room. "You never did tell me how you found Shade."

"I did not?" Rufe appeared surprised.

"Spill it, Rufe. The way things are, ferrying messages is a dangerous job." Jeremiah wasn't bragging; he chose the occupation because it meant the chances of having to kill someone would be less than if he were embroiled in battle.

"I knew Shade when I grew up," Rufe explained. "Pa would not let me near him, because he said no man that mysterious had anything good to give the world."

"So why did you pick him?"

Rufe weighed his words before speaking. "Pa can be one-sided sometimes. He gets something stuck in his head and no one can budge him. Some folks did not think I should get the job of clerk because I am so scatterbrained. But Colonel took a chance on me. It is the best thing that could have happened. I have learned so much that I am almost like a new person, especially working for you."

Rufe was silent for a moment. "I think everyone should get the chance to prove they can do great things. This job does not ask much of Shade except to ride, which he loves, and to stay away from those who might try to stop him, which he is good at doing." Rufe's eyes widened. "You are not going to fire him, are you?"

Jeremiah shook his head. "Shade might be slow, but he does a grand job."

Rufe nodded his head. "Will that be all then? I hoped to help set up for tonight."

Jeremiah straightened some papers. "You go on. I will wait for Shade."

"I sure hope Shade is all right."

"I do, too." Jeremiah recalled Shade's warning that there would be more attacks and that the militia would want to go after the Praying Indians because of them. What would happen if Shade got caught in something and wasn't able to think fast enough to defend himself?

Jeremiah didn't know Shade very well, but he knew the man performed to the best of his ability. In a war, some didn't return; that risk was always there. Jeremiah turned the thought away. He hoped he didn't have to hear that Shade hadn't made it.

Rufe got ready to leave. "If it helps, I am behind you every step of the way, lieutenant."

Jeremiah gave the clerk a small smile. "I do not see how I can miss, then. With you pushing from behind and the Lord pulling me along, seems like I could just about deal with anything."

꿈

Jeremiah gave up after two hours of waiting and headed toward Bessie's to visit his niece. As he neared the Halls', he saw Sarah and Samuel making their way toward him. Jeremiah grinned as Samuel leaped across a puddle.

What a wonderful blessing God provided in the form of children, he thought.

Samuel's mother wasn't bad, either. Sarah's hair cascaded down her back, and her flushed cheeks gave testimony to the length of time she'd been out in the cold. Jeremiah's heart raced. He took a deep breath to calm down, but his heart refused to listen.

A few days after her fainting spell, Sarah had sought him out. She apologized for demanding that Jeremiah not worry about the little people, and admitted that it was probably just a spell of anxiety that caused her to collapse.

While her words were spontaneous, Jeremiah thought he had detected a glimmer of something more beneath the surface. Since then, Jeremiah tried to let Sarah set the terms of their friendship. He did not think he'd gotten very far.

Samuel ran toward him. "Miah! Miah!" He proudly displayed a missing front tooth.

"Hello, scamp!" Jeremiah squatted in front of the boy.

Samuel scuffed the toe of his shoe on the ground.

"What?" Jeremiah exclaimed in mock astonishment. "I know we have not seen each other since little Elizabeth was born, Sammy. Have you forgotten me?"

"I am the only one who calls him Sammy." Sarah pulled her son close to her side. "Come along, Sammy. We promised Bessie we would be right back with the tea."

Jeremiah rested his hands on his knees. Samuel looked as if he wanted to stay but didn't want his mother to know. Jeremiah's heart caught in his throat.

"Go on, Samuel," he encouraged. "Smart men always mind the women in their lives."

"Now that is an interesting admission, coming from you, Mr. Stewart."

Jeremiah met her gaze. "I did not always believe it, but I have discovered that without the love of a good woman, many men fail to accomplish great things."

"And you claim that the same is true for you?"

Jeremiah stood up. "Perhaps I have never had the right woman behind me, one who inspired me to do more than I could alone. . . ."

Sammy pressed against Sarah's side just in time to save her. "Mother? I'm hungry."

"Yes, son. Only a moment longer." She gave Jeremiah a guarded glance.

"You better go," Jeremiah said. "I do not want the little fellow to starve."

"Yes. Bessie will wonder where we are if we are not home soon. Come on, Sammy."

"Sarah?"

"Yes?" She squeezed Sammy's hand.

"I know you recall that a few weeks ago we agreed to try to be friends. I do not feel I have done much to further our friendship, so I would like you to do something for me."

"And that is?"

"Honor me by sitting with me at the Winter Supper."

"See, Mother? Miah wants us. We can go," Sammy offered.

Sarah kept to herself how much Jeremiah's invitation thrilled her. She was tired of mourning, of holding to the past and having it drag her down. And here was a chance to make up to him for what she'd failed to do as a friend in the last few weeks.

"I will go, but you must understand that I go only as your friend."

And because it will keep you from sitting with Gemma Winslow, Sarah thought.

Jeremiah's grin melted any ice that might have remained in Sarah's heart. "I hoped you would say that."

twelve

"If you keep moving, I will never make sure you are proper."

"Quit fussing, Bessie. It is a get-together to listen to Captain's service, eat, then come back here. One would think this is my wedding day, the way you are acting."

"If you would just open your eyes and your heart," Bessie answered, "it could be your wedding day. I must say that you look very fetching in this dress."

Sarah held her tongue as Bessie fiddled with a bunch of material at the back of Sarah's garment. Though Jeremiah had given the cloth to Bessie as a gift, Bessie pressed Sarah into accepting it for all the work Sarah had done for the Halls, both before and after Elizabeth's birth.

Bessie had used one of Sarah's old dresses for the sizing. This wasn't a drab, washer-woman style, and it wasn't the orange-brown material Sarah once had admired at the post. Sarah didn't know how Jeremiah had procured the deep-green fabric, but it made Sarah think of spring leaves, of hope, of a better time.

She glanced down at the gown. Bessie had cut off tiny wooden buttons from one of her old garments, and they marched in two straight lines up each side of the skirt. Full sleeves accented the top of the dress.

"Ouch! That hurt!" Sarah jerked away from the stab of the needle, the skirt frolicking around her ankles. If she only had something more fancy than these plain brown moccasins to wear with it, she would be happy.

"You are as frayed at the edges as some of the seams of this dress." Bessie held up a handful of bits of material she had picked up off the floor.

"I am not nervous," Sarah declared.

Not much, anyway, she admitted to herself. Her heart pounded in her ears at the idea of being around so many people at once. That was all. She was also thirsty, but if she sipped any more water, she'd have to disrobe to relieve herself.

"First is the worship," Bessie reminded her. "Then the feast, with as many of us as can fit into the big room off the store."

"I know. And we are to sit at the commander's table." Sarah wished that thought would quit playing so vividly at the front of her mind.

Bessie stood back and scrutinized Sarah. "Are you going to be all right?"

"Of course," Sarah replied. "I am going tonight only as a friend to Jeremiah. There is nothing between us, and I do not want you thinking that there is."

"You will have a good time."

Bessie's promise was overcome by Samuel's announcement: "Cap'n is fixin' to take us to the supper."

Sammy's eyes sparkled. Sarah knew he expected great things from the evening. In a way, so did she, despite her insistence to Bessie that she was only going as Jeremiah's friend.

≈

A gentle breeze teased the flames of candles set along the edges of the walkway. Frigid temperatures made the sprinkling of stars in the sky shine much brighter than normal. All in all, it appeared for the moment that the settlers' tenuous hold on peace and security was safe.

Some of the men had moved the store furniture out of the way, making room for everyone who brought chairs to line them up. Captain had taken their chairs over earlier.

Inside, lanterns glowed softly, lending a special radiance to the room. Sap snapped in a corner fireplace. Sarah trailed behind Bessie, nodding politely as Captain introduced her to those she had not yet met.

Sarah knew within moments of meeting Gemma Winslow that the encounter was not going to be a high point of Sarah's night.

Gemma's voice dripped with derision. "So you are the one staying with the Halls. Jeremiah told me all about you—and your poor little boy."

Sarah strove to sound pleasant, though she really wanted to shove a handful of snow down Gemma's too-low neckline. "We do not plan on staying here long," she replied. "Washington County is just a temporary solution."

"That is good," Gemma replied. "There is so little here for a widow. All the good men are taken, if you know what I mean."

Sarah knew exactly what Gemma implied, but Sarah was the one who would sit with Jeremiah at the supper. That provided her a small sense of satisfaction. Sarah gave Gemma a cautious glance while Gemma exclaimed over baby Elizabeth. The woman soon moved on to other potential conquests, and, with a sigh, Sarah gazed around.

The entire county appeared to be there. Sarah spent time memorizing the sights so she might pull them out later and, recall the festive details.

Sammy pointed out various small discoveries. For once, Sarah bit back the desire to hush him. He meandered freely between seats where families grinned at his very proper hellos.

After an opening prayer in which he thanked the Lord for the turnout, Captain began to recite the story of the Christ child's birth.

Sarah's Bible readings to Bessie during the last few months had reawakened knowledge Sarah thought long forgotten. Though her mind resisted, Sarah felt God's Word working in her heart. She could not pinpoint a time, but she knew it wouldn't be long until she again believed in God. She looked forward to that day when she could cast off her fears and feast on the promise of eternal life.

Captain's exuberant voice beseeched the crowd not to forget Jesus' sacrifice. As he spoke, the cross at the front of the room drew Sarah's full attention. Comprised of two saplings tied together with strips of leather, it was an amazing sight.

Sarah was struck by the significance that from trees which provided nuts for eating came a symbol that gave so many here a different type of nourishment. Her heart ached as she realized how much she had missed making that connection.

She closed her eyes, thinking that perhaps this was the night when she would allow God back into her life. But a commotion drew Sarah's attention.

She watched as Jeremiah and two other men entered the room. The older one she presumed to be Colonel Williamson. He wore a pair of dark trousers and a well-worn gray shirt. His hair looked as if he had not combed it in a week.

On the other hand, Jeremiah was smartly turned out in a pair of black trousers and a crisp white shirt, one that Sarah was proud to have pressed. Her heart raced. She couldn't help but think how splendid Jeremiah looked. She did not get a good look at the third man as the trio took their seats and the hubbub subsided.

When Captain finished his sermon, Jeremiah rose and apologized for being late. "But," he said, "I have someone with me tonight who has come to impart to us some important news."

"If he means that fool the militia has carrying messages, he belongs in the woodshed, if you ask me," a portly man off to Sarah's left snarled.

Sarah wasn't the only one who thought the comment cruel, as Jeremiah glared at the man before continuing. His gaze rested briefly on Sarah before he went on.

"Many of you are willing to risk your lives in order to keep your families safe," Jeremiah said. "But I have heard comments that place the blame for the atrocities on Indian groups that I do not believe are at fault. I asked Shade, our messenger, to explain some things you may not be aware of."

Shade stood and faced the audience. His dark hair was plaited down his back, and puffy smudges beneath his eyes led one to believe he didn't sleep much.

"Please listen to everything he has to say before you make any judgments," Jeremiah finished.

Shade spoke hesitantly, a fact that several near Sarah grumbled about. Above some rude snorts, he informed the audience about what was happening in the wilds of Ohio and farther west into Illinois. When he offered what he knew about the British encouraging Wyandot warriors to harass the Praying Indians in order to make the Christian tribe look guilty, he gained Sarah's attention. Uneasiness filled her heart.

Shade requested that the audience not blame the Praying Indians. "They serve the same God you worship here tonight," he said. "All they want is to live their lives in peace."

"That ain't true," the portly man near Sarah shouted. "They come over here and kill our folks. You never lost someone to a scalping or you would not be defending those yellow bellies."

Sarah chewed on the inside of her cheek. She really wanted to stand up and tell the blathering idiot to her left what she knew about the Praying Indians. She might have done so, but

Jeremiah sat at the front of the room. She couldn't let him learn about her connection with that tribe.

Shade's features hardened. "I tell you the Praying Indians are not the ones you seek. They are being made to look like they are at fault by those who do not wish to be punished."

"Then who is it?" the man insisted.

A swell of support followed the agitator's comments. Jeremiah stood. The rumble subsided.

"Shade is here at my invitation," he said. "Treat him with respect or you will find I order double details." Jeremiah apologized to Shade.

"It is a sad day, Lieutenant Stewart," Shade said. "As sad a day as when they crucified my Christ."

The portly man erupted again. "You leave Jesus out of this. Those heathens come killin' my family and they will have to reckon with me."

Several shouted their agreement. Jeremiah placed two fingers in his mouth and gave a shrill whistle. The clamor faded.

Shade faced Jeremiah and shrugged. "I cannot change their minds, sir. It is up to you."

❧

Jeremiah later thought that the Winter Supper was one of the worst nights of his life. Sarah left her son with Bessie and disappeared. Jeremiah entertained Samuel willingly, even when Gemma Winslow finagled her way into sitting at his side. He kept glancing at Gemma, wishing that Sarah were sitting there instead.

When he asked, Bessie did not know why Sarah had left early. "Give her time, Jer," she soothed. "Something probably reminded her of her husband, and she needs to sort it all out."

Thanks to the colonel, Jeremiah had at least three more months anyway. He should have turned a deaf ear to Williamson's pleas and refused to serve any longer. He would have, but he kept thinking of Bessie and Captain and their new baby, and Sarah and Samuel. He didn't know what one man could do if Indians attacked, but he felt better knowing he was at least trying to help defend them.

But if he left the militia, then what? Would he leave Washington County? Where would he go? What would he do?

Gemma's nasal tone intruded on Jeremiah's thoughts. "This is absolutely the most wonderful gathering. I do declare, Jeremiah, you went all out to make this evening so special." She batted her eyes.

Jeremiah mumbled his agreement. He didn't feel like talking to Gemma. It would have been much nicer to have Sarah beside him.

"I asked Uncle Davy when he thought he was going to promote you, Jeremiah," Gemma said. "Do you know what his answer was?"

Jeremiah shook his head. He didn't care about promotions. Three months and he'd be gone.

"Well, he said that it would all depend on how soon you and I—"

"Excuse me—sir?"

"Yes, Rufe. What is it?"

"I hate to interrupt, but it is time to go, Lieutenant Stewart." Jeremiah jumped up, rapidly excusing himself.

"Will you be back soon?" Gemma's anxious tone followed him out the door.

ᕤ

Sarah tucked Sammy into bed, avoiding Bessie's questions. Once he fell asleep, she flung her dress into a corner. Myriad emotions prompted by Shade's earlier comments battered her.

No matter how she tried, Sarah couldn't remember Shade's exact words. Was he for or against the Praying Indians? Sarah thought he'd tried to convince the gathering to believe that the

Christian Indians should not be blamed for any killings in Washington County.

Jeremiah said he invited Shade to speak at the supper. Did that mean Jeremiah didn't believe the Praying Indians were guilty? Perhaps Jeremiah had attempted to get Sarah to tell him about the Indians because he thought that he could stop the militia from attacking them.

Sarah scrunched her eyes shut. If she could just recall exactly what Shade had said, she'd be able to figure it out. One thing was for sure—the crowd did not agree that the Praying Indians were innocent.

Realizing she would not figure it out tonight, Sarah sighed and climbed onto her mat. She gave one last glance toward the dark corner where her gown lay. So much for dreams.

Sleep eluded her. Her mind returned again and again to Jeremiah. Would he arrive in the morning and demand to know why she had left the gathering? Sarah balled her hands into fists. If Jeremiah learned that she had grown up with the Indians that most militia members apparently thought responsible for destroying their families, then Jeremiah, as part of that company, would want nothing to do with her.

Fear pooled in Sarah's heart. Not long ago she admitted to him that she traveled with a missionary to live in the Ohio wilderness. At the time, she did not suspect that Jeremiah would connect that missionary with the Praying Indians.

Shade's comments left no doubt that Jeremiah would eventually make that link. While he might be able to accept her despite her having lived with Indians at one time, Sarah did not think Jeremiah would accept her if he learned what she had done eight years ago.

Why is that? a little voice in her mind nagged.

"Because I do not want to hurt Jeremiah," Sarah whispered. "I care about him. As a friend doing a job he does not want to do in this wilderness we live in."

Is that all? the tiny voice quizzed.

No, but I will just have to deal with the way I feel about Jeremiah as a man. On my own. Again.

❧

At the last possible moment, Sarah led Sammy down the hall to the eating room. She convinced herself that any unpleasantness about her disappearance from the assembly last night was better off dealt with and put behind her.

Captain's blessing was quick. "Bless this food to nourish our bodies. And pass the flatcakes, Bessie."

The ping of forks against pewter plates and the soft thud of wooden mugs being set on the tabletop accompanied other normal eating sounds. Sarah waited for Captain or Bessie to bring up her behavior of the night before.

"Jeremiah is gone," Captain announced after he devoured a towering stack of flatcakes and two mugs of coffee.

Bessie's shocked gaze collided with Sarah's. "When did he leave?"

"Early this morning," Captain said. "Rufe mentioned as we left last night that Jeremiah and some of the others in the militia will be out of the territory for at least a week."

A quick sigh of relief fell from Sarah's lips. Jeremiah would not be coming by to call her to task for running out on him. She drizzled syrup on her flatcakes, but she didn't think she would eat.

"Sarah," Captain began. "I hope you will forgive me for intruding, but I think it is time we talked."

The nibble of food Sarah took stuck in her throat. She glanced between Bessie and Captain. Bessie stayed quiet, as if she wished she knew a way to turn the conversation in another direction.

Sarah realized that she was not the only one who had been

going through rough times. Dull shadows beneath Bessie's eyes were not only because Elizabeth refused to sleep for longer than a few hours. Sarah lost track of the nights Bessie fretted when Captain did not return home when Bessie expected him to. Even when he did, he rose early to visit with families whose men had joined the militia and were having second thoughts.

A feeling of hollowness invaded Sarah as she shoved her plate aside. "I suppose it is. First, please allow me to apologize for last night. My behavior was highly unsuitable."

"I think you should save your apology for Jeremiah when he returns," Captain said. "I wish to speak to you about something else."

"Oh? But I thought. . ."

Captain cleared his throat. "This is not easy, not just because of who you are, but because some people believe sharing things of this nature isn't done unless the one addressed is in their immediate family."

"Go on." Sarah could not figure out where he was headed.

"Bessie and I promised not to press you because we realize that everyone heals differently. Neither of us wishes to make you more uncomfortable than you already are."

"Just say whatever it is you wish to say," Sarah stated. "You do not have to go slowly with me. I am strong enough to stand up to anything." She placed her hands in her lap, pressing her right thumb into her left palm.

Captain scratched at his beard. "I understand that you are helping Bessie learn her letters. Some would say that is a good work, Sarah, something that she will have with her the rest of her life."

"Did you not want her to learn?" Sarah wondered if she'd upset Captain without realizing it.

"No. I am glad you are doing it. But that is not my point."

Sammy played with his flatcake, pushing it around his plate and saying, "Gee-up, gee-up." He'd seen the militiamen say that to their mounts. Sarah laid a hand on his arm to stop him. He sulked but began to eat without any accompanying sounds.

A compassionate smile softened Captain's face. "Sometimes we make choices that we think are best based on our circumstances at the time. Now and then, even though we regret them, we maintain those decisions because we think there is no way out, or because we are afraid to admit that we made a mistake."

"I do not follow you," Sarah commented. "How does that apply to me?" Beneath the table, she began squeezing her hands together.

"Pray take this in the spirit with which I give it," Captain went on. "I am here to serve any who need it. I often speak with men who are being asked to do things they never imagined they would have to do. Many of them were raised without God. They are the most challenging to convince that if they ask Jesus into their hearts, He will heal their troubled souls. Not all accept that immediately. Sadly, some choose to ignore everything I say."

Sarah's mind whirled at his words. "Are you telling me that if I go back to Jesus, all my troubles will disappear?"

Captain's voice was firm. "Trials and tribulations never disappear completely. But I do know that since you lost your husband, you seem to have chosen to live without tapping into God's power. What I want you to think about is this, Sarah: How much more could you do if you had Him on your side again?"

thirteen

"Ya got tha wrong place, mister, if yore lookin' for dem Prayin' Indians. Da Brits dragged 'em all off las' fall."

Jeremiah studied the scraggly figure who said his name was Mash. He reeked of vinegar and a month without bathing. He also had a habit of picking his teeth while he talked, which jumbled his words.

Jeremiah had ridden hard in order to arrive in the Muskingum Valley in just over a day and a half. He would ride just as hard on the return trip, but not before he discovered what he could about these mission settlements carved into the Ohio wilds.

"Can you tell me anything about them, or their missionaries?"

"Don' know what 'twould be." A scowl formed along the edges of Mash's unshaven lips.

Jeremiah motioned toward the settlement. "I can tell this place was not always like this. It took some effort and time to build such log homes. It is too bad they have been allowed to deteriorate so much."

Standing at the entrance, Jeremiah could see more than forty cabins, their walls bonded with chinking. Their roofs sloped sharply toward the ground, a necessary slant that encouraged winter snow to slide off. A fence, woven around the bottom portion with dried grapevine, rambled down two sides of the mission behind the rows of homes, but portions of it were missing.

"Don't matter ta us. We're deserters from da British army. Also got some Indians who claim ta be our allies. We didn't have nowhere else ta go and dis was available." Mash spit out the pieces of bark from a twig he'd been chewing. "I only been here a few weeks. Rode in, got 'vited to share some whiskey, and ain't never left. Can't tell ya nothin' 'cause I don't know nothin'." Mash paused to wipe spittle from his beard. "Ain't got nothin' ta give, I ain't."

"I will ride on then," Jeremiah said. "I appreciate your taking the time to speak with me." He shivered as he realized how different Mash's greeting would be if he discovered Jeremiah was on an official militia scouting trip.

Someone shouted from down the pathway. "Mash! Get yore backside over here so ya can finish da cookin'."

Mash waved off the shout. "Ya best be ridin' on if dat's yore plan."

"That is my plan." Jeremiah was glad he didn't have to stay around these ruffians. They made his skin crawl. They didn't do much for his appetite either. He turned his horse toward the tree line.

Should he go farther? He knew there was another settlement downriver, one with a name Jeremiah could never remember how to pronounce. What would he prove by going there? Likely he'd find the same hopeless sort living among homes that were once filled with prayer and praise.

Jeremiah clucked his tongue. His mount moved forward. Before horse and rider blended into the tree cover, Jeremiah took a last look back at the mission. He tried to see the settlement as it once must have been, tried to decide which of the homes might have been Sarah's.

❧

"I am tired of talking about it, Bessie."

Sarah dropped the stack of plates onto the table, hoping their clatter would get her point across. She didn't want to hear about Jeremiah, or the past, or her future.

"You cannot quit because you are tired," Bessie pleaded.

"Someday you will have to face what is ahead of you, Sarah. That means you are going to have to let go of the past."

Sarah glanced out a small window to see Captain showing Sammy how to push a pine branch at the snow to clear their walkway.

"I have faced Levi's death, Bessie. Why do you think I brought Sammy here? I want to make life better for him."

"I will grant you that. You have done everything you can to make his life easier. But I have one final thing to say."

"Then please do so. I need to get to work mending Sammy's britches."

"If you faced Levi's death, Sarah, then you should now think about your own." Bessie settled her arms across her still-pudgy middle.

Sarah's eyes widened. "My own? Why, that is the most ridiculous notion I have ever heard. I do not plan on dying for years."

"None of us do, Sarah," Bessie rejoined. "Sometimes it happens earlier than we expect. Levi is a good example of that. You read to me the other night from Hebrews chapter nine. Remember? You read that it is appointed unto men to die once then to face the judgment. We both know that God numbers the hairs on our heads, we just do not know when it will be our turn. That is why you have to be ready to explain to God why you turned from Him and insisted on running things on your own."

Sarah thought about Bessie's comments. "You are right, Bessie. A few years ago, when I trusted God, I was happier. Then disaster struck, taking with it my faith—in God and humankind. I long to be the open and caring person of yesteryear, but I am not sure how to go about it."

"Happiness takes effort, Sarah. So does living when you think there is no reason to go on. God gives us heartaches to make us stronger. If we never weep, how can we know what true love really is?"

Sarah tucked a wayward strand of hair behind her ear. "God gave His only Son as a measure of how much He loved the world He created, as a sign of His trust that humans would make the right choices in their own lives."

Bessie's eyes glimmered with tears much like Sarah's. "Yes, Sarah. He did."

ॐ

Sarah began to pray daily for Jeremiah's safety. She was not sure that she would ever tell him what she had done eight years ago, nor if he would listen if she tried. But she wanted to do so, for Sarah now knew that she wanted more from Jeremiah Stewart than friendship.

ॐ

Jeremiah frowned as his rap on the door went unanswered. Since thoughts of Sarah had filled his mind on his most recent trip, he was determined to discover why. Journeys through Indian land were dangerous enough without thoughts of a woman clouding his thinking. Once and for all Jeremiah planned to settle the pull Sarah had on him and get her out of his mind.

Gemma Winslow, with all her faults, might not be such a bad choice. At least he didn't spend his free time thinking about Gemma, which allowed him to accomplish what he could for the militia.

"Why, Jeremiah. You are the last person I expected to see. Come in."

He last had seen Sarah leaving the supper before Shade finished speaking. She did not act now as if she were trying to hide anything from him.

Jeremiah knew he must deal with that issue eventually, but for now he spoke as candidly as he could. "I came because there is something I have to get straight."

"I figured as much." Sarah waved him in, her eyes betraying an uneasiness at his presence.

"Is Bessie here?"

"She had a touch of stomach trouble yesterday, but I think she might be well enough to get up. Let me get her."

"No. I came to speak with you on official business. Can we sit down?"

He heard Sarah inhale sharply, but she followed him to the eating room.

Sarah spent some time arranging her skirt folds after she took her seat. "Go on and have your say," she finally said without looking at him.

Jeremiah draped his hat over the top prong of the chair. "I am not good at easing into things carefully, so I want you to know that anything I say is not designed as an attack on you."

He laid his hands palms down on the table, staring at a scar on the bridge of his knuckles. He had received the wound when he pummeled a tree shortly after learning about Jenny's death.

"You are not making much sense, Jeremiah."

"Nothing makes sense anymore, Sarah. I pray daily, begging God to provide the answers I need to do what is best. You once ordered me to forget about the little people. I did not even try, because I know I cannot do that. I might not like my position in the militia, but the little people are young boys like your Samuel, and like my niece Elizabeth. They are the families, friends, and people I see daily, even you. They are also our enemies, many of whom have no more choice in what is going on than we do. Sometimes it seems things are more confused than they ought to be."

"I thought you said you came here to discuss business."

Jeremiah sighed. "When I first took this job, I worried

about learning everything I had to do."

"So?"

"I have prayed more in the last ten months than I have ever done in my life," he admitted.

"You must be lacking sleep, for you are talking in circles." Sarah's glance flitted past Jeremiah's and ended up on the woodpile.

"No, Sarah. It is not from lack of sleep. It is more likely because, when I think of you or look at you, words seem to flee my mind. Speaking sensibly becomes one of the hardest things I have ever had to do."

Sarah shifted position. "I do not think that is why you are really here. Is it, Mr. Stewart?"

Jeremiah drummed his fingertips against the tabletop. The fact that she had not used his given name hurt, but he ignored it. "You are right. You once told me you traveled with a missionary after the orphanage you lived in was destroyed."

Sarah raised her chin to look him squarely in the eye. "That is true."

"I am making an assumption here that may be incorrect, but did you happen to settle in the eastern part of Ohio?"

Only the continual drumming of his fingers on the table broke the silence. Jeremiah watched as fear flickered in Sarah's eyes.

"There is nothing I know of that says a person cannot move around wherever they wish, is there?"

"No, but I need to hear what you know about it."

"The mission?"

Jeremiah didn't know exactly what he was looking for. He'd seen the settlement with his own eyes. "Where it is. How many lived there. What kind of land surrounds it. Tell me anything you can think of."

Sarah jumped up and tramped around the small room.

Jeremiah cleared his throat. "Several months ago, when I served as a courier, I met most of the Indians that David Zeisberger had living with him in those mission settlements."

Sarah glared at him. Jeremiah would have preferred not to continue, but something he didn't understand forced him to go on.

"On this latest trip I stopped by Fort Pitt on my way home," he said.

Sarah pulled at her ear lobe. "So?"

"The commander granted me access to the fort's journals. Those chronicles contained some of Zeisberger's actual missives to those who ran Fort Pitt throughout the last ten years or so."

Sarah's facial expression gave away nothing. "And?"

"In a letter eight years ago, Zeisberger mentioned that one of the young women he allowed to live at the mission disappeared. . .with a young man. . .Levi Lyons." Jeremiah tried not to sound harsh, but the accusation poured out of him.

Sarah paled. "Are you pestering me so that I will confess?"

Jeremiah fought for self-control. "I want to know about the mission. That is all."

&

Sarah studied Jeremiah. His long hair was uncombed, his lips pinched, and she thought he'd lost weight since she'd last seen him. "You want information from me to help you fight your battles with the Indians. Check your muster rolls, Mr. Stewart. I am not one of your soldiers."

Jeremiah threw his hands up in the air. "You have to tell me, Sarah. Why can you not see that?"

"Because I see a greedy man who wants me to help him kill Indians."

"I do not want the information for that reason."

"Oh? You know, Jeremiah, while you were gone I began to

hope that you and I might someday become real friends."

Jeremiah took a step toward her. "I would like to discuss the friendship possibility later. This is official, remember?"

"Right. I did not mean to detain you from your militia business."

"Sarah, I do not want to do it, but I have to tell you that the missionaries and inhabitants of those missions are charged with treason."

Sarah did not blink.

"And that the British forced several Praying Indians north, away from their homes, their crops, and their freedom. All I am trying to do is find a way to keep them from being held accountable for something they probably have not done."

Sarah remained silent, but agitation flashed in her eyes.

"I am a Christian, Sarah. I do not kill people on purpose. My parents taught me to love all mankind, not just those with the same color skin as mine."

The growing sparks in Sarah's eyes were the only indication that she heard him.

"Do you not see?" Jeremiah pushed on. "I chose to deliver messages because I refused to take an active part in killing people."

"You are not carrying letters back and forth any longer," Sarah accused. "You are even more involved in the decisions to send men out after them. You might as well murder them with your own hands."

"You feel strongly about this because you knew people at that mission, and there are others in places near them that you knew, too."

"That is not. . .the reason!"

"Then tell me why you keep refusing to cooperate," Jeremiah demanded. "What is it that bothers you about Schoenbrunn, or that other place, Ja-nade-en?"

"Ja-nadd-den-hut-ten," Sarah said, correcting his mispronunciation of the Christian settlement Gnadenhutten. "You would not understand."

"You do not know that. You are judging me without knowing what drives me," Jeremiah stated. "You have not given me a chance since the very first time we met, have you? You are afraid of commitments, Sarah. That is what this boils down to."

"That is not true."

"You are too afraid that what we share now might grow into something significant, are you not?"

Sarah dropped her gaze to the floor. Her heart twisted in the wrong direction, hurting much as it had when renegades had killed her husband. That couldn't be. There was only one man she loved that much, and his name was *not* Jeremiah Stewart.

"I do not have to know you to see what sort of man you are. I have met others like you."

"You have not been listening to me, Sarah. I keep trying to tell you that I am not like the other men you have known."

"Really? Then why are you, like everyone else, unable to understand that there are some things about my life that I do not wish to share? Keeping it hidden is much easier to deal with, so much less painful."

"That is fine with me. But at least tell me what type of man I am, Sarah Lyons. I want to hear it from you."

Sarah lifted her chin, meeting his gaze. "This is ridiculous. This is not business, as you professed it was to be when you arrived, nor is it getting us anywhere."

Jeremiah pretended not to understand the hurt in Sarah's eyes. "We will not get anywhere until you let someone knock that frown from your face and that pain out of your heart. I have been there, Sarah. I know what it feels like."

"You do not have any inkling of what happened to me, Jeremiah."

"I can tell that you lost something very precious."

"As if you would understand the agony in that," Sarah said.

"Yes, I w—"

Jeremiah's words were lost in Bessie's worried interruption. "What is going on in here?" Bessie bumbled into the room, rubbing her eyes. "I heard voices." She glanced back and forth between the two of them. "If this is private, I will leave."

"It is not private," Jeremiah volunteered when Sarah said nothing.

"No. It is not," Sarah granted. "I was just telling your brother farewell."

Bessie slipped to Jeremiah's side and gave him a sisterly hug. "Welcome back, Jer. Did you know you two were making enough noise to scare a herd of wild horses away?"

Jeremiah and Sarah glowered at each other.

Jeremiah jerked his head toward Sarah. "I came over because Sarah knows things about those missions that Zeisberger settled in the Muskingum valley. She refuses to help."

"For a very good reason," Sarah inserted. She wasn't about to be outdone by a headstrong man. She was gaining her independence and no one was going to take it away from her.

"Sarah, you have to put your own feelings aside for the moment," Jeremiah cajoled. "You might know something that will help avoid a disaster. That alone should make a difference."

Sarah crossed her arms in front of her, not caring that it drew attention to her shaking shoulders. "I have not been there in years."

"That does not matter. Tell me what you know about the people who lived there. How strong was their faith? Why did they choose that area?"

"Both of you can ask all that you want, but I will not divulge a thing."

"Jer?" Bessie stood beside her brother, though she appeared to want to be at both their sides. "Give Sarah some time. Knowing you, you sprang this on her and now you have her all worked up. I am sure that once Sarah mulls it over, she will realize that helping you is the right thing to do."

Sarah faced Bessie. "Do not tell me that you think I should assist him?"

"Eventually Jeremiah will get the information from somewhere. If you know something, Sarah, why not tell him now? It might help keep us all safer here. You do not want something to happen to Samuel, do you?"

It made no sense, but Sarah ignored the plea for Sammy's safety. She'd vowed never to let a man have any power over her. If she told Jeremiah even a bit of what she knew, he would come back for more.

"I do not trust what he is going to do with it," Sarah stated.

"I am trying to help those people, Sarah," Jeremiah responded. "You have to believe me."

"I have known Jeremiah all my life," Bessie said to Sarah. "Not once did he ever lie to me or let me down. You can depend on him." She turned back to her brother. "Sarah is not going to tell you today. Let her sort things out."

Sort things out? Did Bessie think that what Sarah felt was as simple as sorting the whites from the darks for the wash? It was much more complicated than that.

"I do not need time." Sarah glanced between them. "I will not tell anyone about the Moravians."

"What if it means you might save their lives, Sarah?" Jeremiah prodded. "Will you still keep it to yourself?"

"I might."

He dropped a fist onto the table. Bessie winced.

"All right, then," Jeremiah declared. "I will not ask you again. Human life obviously does not mean much to you."

"It means a lot to me." Sarah faltered. "It does. Truly."

"Then prove it by putting others ahead of yourself for once." Jeremiah flung the words at her as he thrust his arms through his jacket sleeves.

His reluctance to probe further made Sarah wish she had confided something to him, even if it was one small tidbit— just so she knew he would come back to see her.

fourteen

"I do not know how much more I can take." Jeremiah shoved Shade's latest delivery aside and threw his hands over his face. He cared little that he looked nothing like a man of battle.

"What now?" Rufe asked respectfully.

Jeremiah shrugged. "I knew there would be trouble when I learned that British commander ordered those Praying Indians from their homes last fall."

"You cannot change that, sir."

Jeremiah straightened a stack of papers. "I know, but things are getting worse. I have a feeling that something is about to happen, and we are not going to like the result."

Rufe slumped into a chair. "Pretty much what Shade tried to tell everyone at the Winter Supper. So what are you going to do? You cannot run to Fort Detroit. It is a British holding, and I have heard that their commander is the best they have."

Jeremiah pondered things for a moment. "Perhaps Shade can find out more about what is going on."

Rufe sat up. "To prove what?"

"I do not know," Jeremiah confessed. "I have already made one trip there, but sending Shade beats sitting here waiting for something or someone to come to us. Williamson promised I would only serve till mid-March. He said he would not ask me to take Dan Whelp's place. Well, it has been over a month and a half, and he has yet to submit a replacement name for the major's position!"

"Colonel Williamson is a busy man." Rufe clearly did not want to take sides with either Williamson or Jeremiah.

"Busy rounding up more men for his militia," Jeremiah scoffed. "Sometimes I think he moves people into the county so that he will have more men on the rolls."

Rufe propped a finger under his chin. "Perhaps you could send a message to headquarters insisting that they appoint someone. Never mind. You already tried that."

"God put me here to do something, Rufe. I just do not know what." Jeremiah ran his hands through his hair.

"Pa always says we should not bring trouble upon ourselves," Rufe stated. "He says we should look for what we can do that is good and be satisfied with that."

Jeremiah fanned the edges of the papers. "Your pa is a smart man, Rufe, but that does not ease my frustration."

"What if we send someone out to get Colonel back here? Then you could demand that he do something about replacing Dan Whelp. That is what you want, is it not?"

"Yes. No. I do not know. I am worried we are going to find ourselves being attacked by more Indians than we can handle. If that happens, we will have no choice but to defend ourselves, to kill." Jeremiah raised stricken eyes to the clerk. "That is strictly between you and me."

"Yes, sir," Rufe promised.

"That must be so," Jeremiah replied. "For if anyone found out how I feel, I might be looking at a charge of treason."

❧

Winter slipped by in a barrage of blizzards and icy winds. Sarah hadn't seen Jeremiah since they quarreled about the mission. Early on, each day she expected him to visit and question her further, but he never did.

Did she miss him? Kick a squirrel in the tail and chase it up a tree. Why would she miss Jeremiah? She should be glad he no longer dropped by as he once had. But the short winter days made for long nights, times when Sarah thought about

Jeremiah and Gemma. . .together.

Sarah turned her mind to happier prospects. Bessie and Sammy's "letter lessons" were going well. Bessie had caught on quickly to the shapes of the letters of the alphabet. Sammy ran a close second with his ability to recite the letters in sequence.

Sarah knew that on days when the snow wasn't blowing too hard or the wind too chilly, Bessie bundled up and went to visit her brother. Sometimes Sarah allowed Bessie to take Sammy along. Other times Bessie went alone, leaving baby Elizabeth, or Lizzie as she was now known, with Sarah.

Sammy loved to sit beside Sarah as she held Lizzie, babbling and smiling at the infant. Sarah felt her heart warm when Lizzie charmed her with a toothless grin.

Sarah refused to ask about Jeremiah, knowing it would only lead Bessie to speculate about her motives for asking. One day, though, Sarah couldn't hide her curiosity any longer. She waited until Bessie had put away her purchases from the post.

"Is this a busy time of year for the militia?" Sarah hoped her use of the term "militia" disguised her true interest.

"Jeremiah is always a busy man." Bessie failed to hide her smug grin. "Do you miss seeing him?"

"About as much as I miss those oxen that pulled our wagon here," Sarah quipped.

"I wish you two would work out your problems. Jer is just as troubled as you are. I am sure it is because he feels you no longer care to see him."

"He is free to think that if he wishes." Sarah hoped Bessie did not mention Gemma Winslow, for Sarah didn't think she could take hearing that woman's name.

Toward February's end a huge snowfall left them homebound and impatient for the white stuff to melt. Captain read from the Bible, encouraging Bessie to try out the words she knew. Bessie's hesitant, but progressively improving, attempts gave Sarah a great feeling of accomplishment.

Sarah grew used to seeing Sammy climb up on Captain's knee, as if it were the most natural thing in the world for Sammy to do. She enjoyed listening as Captain explained Jesus and the apostles to her son.

Captain left without explanation one afternoon. Bessie fretted until he returned with a goose. He stated the gift came from a family who wished to express their appreciation to him for sharing the gospel with them.

Bessie basted the goose with cream and hung it over the hearth. The aroma of sizzling fowl filtered through the home throughout the night. Sarah slept soundly until she was jolted awake by early spring's gusty breath lifting the roof edges and dropping them back into place.

As Sarah waited for a pan of sugared bread to finish frying, Captain entered the room. At first he said nothing. Sarah remained quiet while he flipped through his Bible. She watched as he picked up the locket of hair she had dropped that day months ago. He ran a finger along its length, then flipped the pages.

Sarah swallowed hard. "Captain?"

It seemed an eternity before he glanced at her. "Good morning, Sarah. Did you sleep well?"

"Until the racket began outside."

Captain chuckled. "Those northern blasts can be quite chilling. Did you need something?"

His cheeks were plumper than Sarah had noticed recently, and though his hair appeared grayer, the youthful echo of auburn peppered his beard.

Sarah explained her clumsiness with the tuft of hair a few months earlier. "I am so sorry. I should have told you long ago. I thought Bessie already had."

Captain arched an eyebrow. "Isaiah 40 or 41?"

"Forty."

"The Lord works in mysterious ways," Captain said. "I chose Proverbs, but Isaiah is just as appropriate."

"I am not sure how you expect me to answer that," Sarah answered. "You know my faith is not exactly a shining example for others to follow."

"God's Word contains beautiful promises, no matter where you look," Captain said. "And I think you are wrong, Sarah. I feel that what happened to you was of such size that it overwhelmed you. You would not be the first to turn away from God during disaster."

"Are you saying I never quit putting my faith in God? I hardly think that is true. Look at what He did to my family. Everyone seems to forget that."

"We have not forgotten, Sarah. More than likely it is that we suffered something that pains us just as deeply, but we accepted it and prefer to look ahead, not backward."

Sarah lived with her disappointments and lost dreams every day. "I keep seeing that. . .night. . .happening over and over. I will never forget it."

Captain nodded. "I had trouble, too, until I decided to set aside a block of time each day and use that to deal with my pain. Eventually I taught myself to push the ache away until the next day."

"Seems to me," Sarah replied, "that if I made myself think about it every day on purpose, I would just recall it more."

"There is that risk, but if you truly want to become a mother that Samuel is proud of, then each day you work at making yourself think of the hurt less. You will never forget it completely, though—it is too much a part of you."

"What if I never put. . .it. . .behind me?" Sarah closed her eyes, wishing that the choices she'd made had not turned out to be so disastrous.

"You think that if you put your pain behind you, you will also put your husband there." Captain fingered the small lock of hair. "It might be hard for you to understand right now, but someday Levi will be separate in your mind from the pain."

"How do you know that?" Sarah's question filled the room.

Captain smiled. "This clip of hair came from my first wife's curls. We were not blessed with children, but I loved her, still do in my own private way. No one can ever take that from me. Katherine is gone, but she lives on in my heart. Every time a robin sings, I hear her voice, feel her love, touch again the gentle waves of her beautiful red hair."

Captain fingered the lock of hair. Sarah grasped the edge of her apron. Finally, Captain cleared his throat, brushing aside the solemn moment. "It does not make me love Bessie any less. In fact, it took me a while to realize that if I did not know the great trust that comes with loving God, if Katherine had not been abruptly taken from me, I might have missed out on Bessie and little Lizzie."

He hung his head, hiding his tears. "And that would have been a real shame."

fifteen

Captain's disclosure explained the inscription in his Bible that Sarah had read months ago. It also played heavily on her heart over the next few days. While Sarah didn't wish to snoop, she did want to discover more about how Captain relinquished the grief associated with losing his first wife. And, she recalled, hadn't Bessie hinted at something similar?

Speaking of Bessie, Sarah noticed that she no longer flitted about and chirped inane things as she once had done. Bessie was now an earnest young woman, devoted to raising her daughter as best she could in troubled times. Sarah found that she missed the constant chatter Bessie once had filled the days with. She decided one afternoon to have a talk with Bessie, to see if she could learn why she'd changed.

Her plans were stymied. Bessie came down with a cold. Captain stayed at his wife's side constantly, refusing to allow even Sarah to tend to Bessie. Sarah recalled how Levi always had taken care of her when she was ill. Thinking of him now didn't cause her as much pain as it usually did. She'd begun doing as Captain had suggested and hoped this was a sign of progress.

After Bessie recovered, Sarah waited until Captain left for a visit to a neighbor's home before she began the conversation.

Bessie searched Sarah's face as if looking for a clue. "I knew you needed something of me. What is it you want to know?"

Sarah swallowed. "For one thing, how do you always know I am troubled?"

Bessie spoke without hesitation. "Not long after you joined us, I learned that when you are not—shall we say *bothered?*— by something, you are more willing to talk. When something troubles you, you push everyone away except Samuel. . . . That is not what you really want to know, though, is it?"

Sarah shook her head. "I think you seem very different since Lizzie's birth."

"For the better?"

"Yes, but it is also as if there is something deep inside that you cannot resolve," Sarah replied. "I do not mean to pry, but is that true?"

Bessie sighed. "It might sound odd, but having a child scares me, Sarah. Suddenly there is this little lass who depends on me for everything. I did not know it would be so awesome."

"The responsibility?"

Bessie shook her head. "The love. I fell for Captain practically the moment I met him at a worship service—silly me, mooning over a man of God almost twice my age." Bessie chuckled, then sobered. "This is a different sort of caring. You have Samuel, so you know what I mean."

Sarah nodded. That grand tenderness that filled her heart every time she looked at him, the love that was a constant part of her life but sometimes frightened her—different from the passion with which she had loved his father, but just as strong.

"A child is fulfilling," Sarah concurred. "And I am blessed that I did not lose Sammy. He is so full of joy and life that the world seems made just for him to discover. Last night I realized that even though I lost Levi, I still have a part of him with me in Sammy."

"I have said this before," Bessie added. "Samuel will grow up to be a fine man, thanks to your guidance. You let him join Captain as he reads God's Word. That is a wise decision."

"Yes, it seems more intelligent every day. I did some

thinking, Bessie, and it will not do any good if Sammy learns the history of God's people and the plan of salvation if I do not reinforce it."

Bessie simply smiled, and Sarah turned her mind to the men who volunteered to leave their families, if needed, to fight battles they might never return from. And to Captain, who spread the news of redemption regardless of people's reaction to it—Sarah's included. Her thoughts returned to Bessie, who quietly displayed her own brand of hope as she rocked her wee daughter.

Finally, Sarah pondered Jeremiah—tall, confident Jeremiah Stewart. From the beginning he seemed intent on upsetting her tiny fragment of the world. Was he really? Or was that what Sarah thought because she could not believe he really wanted to help her?

No matter what Jeremiah did, Sarah pushed him away because he frightened her. Was it him or was it that when she saw him, she felt things she had resolved she would never allow her heart to feel again?

Sarah shook her head. Bessie was chattering. She rolled her mind away from Jeremiah to listen.

". . .and I told Captain that was the most beautiful thing he could ever say to me."

Sarah apologized for daydreaming.

Bessie gave her a curious look. "Captain said that if it had not been for me, he would not have understood God's plan for his life. He also said that if not for you, Sarah, he would not have shared that with me."

"What did *I* do?"

"Captain told me about how much he once loved Katherine. In all this time, he had never talked about her with me. He said that as he spoke with you, he grew convinced that when you tucked that snippet of hair away, you had chosen Isaiah without realizing it. He believes that the message of hope and comfort that speaks across the years from the prophet Isaiah called to you, asking you to place your trust in the Lord."

"Captain thinks that?"

"And much more," Bessie continued. "That is when he told me the rest. Seems that when we met, he decided to wed me because he thought I would be a help to him spreading the gospel. I do not know why, since I was hardly a good example of the perfect preacher's wife."

Bessie grew pensive, her eyes drifting to Captain's Bible on the mantle. "I suppose I did not truly love him at first," she admitted. "I cared about him and liked him as a friend, but I think I was agog over his good looks and the way he made me feel special."

Good looks? Heavens, Bessie must be blind!

Sarah's taste ran more to men like Jeremiah, men with a hint of danger and an air of greatness about them, yet with a portion of gentleness that shone through at the most unexpected times.

"Why did you wed Captain then?" Sarah challenged.

"I lost my first husband in a farming accident. Martin and I had had big dreams for our future, plans for a large family, and a big farm our boys would help us run. One day he went out to plow and did not come home."

Bessie's eyes filled with tears. She tightened her jaw and went on. "With no one to take care of me, I went back to live with my parents. Jeremiah was there. He had just lost Jenny. I do not have to tell you what a sorrowful bunch we were. Well, Captain came by a few weeks later to stay with us, for my parents held the church service that month."

"How long did you know him before you joined him in wedlock?"

"A few weeks." Bessie caught Sarah's glance of shock. "He was in a hurry to depart for another town. I was in as big a rush to leave home so that my parents would stop telling me they had known all along that Martin had not been right for me."

"It does sound sudden," Sarah murmured.

"Yes, but it has been worth it. I am a blessed woman, Sarah. But only because I accepted what God gave me as my lot in life."

"Can I tell you my story?"

At Bessie's nod, Sarah spoke. "I suppose my departure from Schoenbrunn with Levi was just as impulsive. We were enthusiastic about beginning our lives together. To stay at the mission would mean waiting until the elders, my sister, and his parents decided we could wed."

"Is that all?"

"No. I guess we should have done things differently, but Levi had just lost a niece. He suggested we leave immediately so that he could put some distance between that grief and himself. I went with him because I loved him. After we married, he promised to take care of me until his final day. As you know, that day occurred much earlier than we planned. You and Captain were smart to grasp what joy you could, Bessie. I envy you."

"Someday you will find another," Bessie said. "He may not be what you think you want, but he will fill your heart with his presence. He will draw you into his life without hesitation because he cares about you, perhaps even more than he realizes. If you give him the chance, he will change your life forever."

Sarah raised her eyebrows. "I take it you mean Jeremiah?"

Bessie nodded.

"I do not think there is much of a chance for that, Bessie. Not with Gemma Winslow around."

✍

"Jeremiah is coming to eat with us." Bessie passed on the news and went to her room to nurse Lizzie.

Sarah set the table, then hurried to change dresses. She hadn't seen Jeremiah since the day that she refused to offer him any knowledge she had of the missions. Was it possible he missed her and was coming over to see her?

Drivel! She must be turning soft from sitting around and doing nothing. Even with Rufe coming by in the evenings so that Sarah could teach him his letters, she didn't have much to occupy otherwise empty hours. Sammy played by himself so much, sometimes Sarah wondered if it were normal.

Who could she ask such a question? With Lizzie so young, Bessie wouldn't know what a child should do at Sammy's age. Who then? Sarah hadn't gone out of her way to foster a relationship with any of the women who lived near them. In fact, Sarah realized with a start, Bessie hadn't either.

Why not? Sarah concluded that despite Bessie's insistence otherwise, she must be ashamed of having Sarah and Sammy living with them. Well, Sarah couldn't change that now, but in the spring she would think about moving on. She'd said this move to Washington County was only temporary in any case.

Sarah donned the dress made from the emerald material. With the full skirt swirling around her ankles, she moved down the hallway, her heart pounding at the sound of Jeremiah's voice.

Sarah listened from the hall as he entertained Bessie and Sammy with tales of something Rufe had told him. They quieted as she arrived.

"Do not stop because of me," Sarah said, giving each of them a smile.

"We are not." Jeremiah rose and motioned for her to take his seat.

Sarah gazed at Jeremiah. If she left in search of her sister, she would never see him again. A part of her heart splintered. If only things had worked out differently. . .

"I did not get a chance to tell you before, but your dress looks grand." Jeremiah's gaze swept the smooth lines of her gown.

He was, of course, referring to the night she had fled the supper wearing this same garment. Why did she think he would not raise that topic eventually?

Sarah seated herself where she did not have to look directly at Jeremiah. "I have never apologized for leaving that night. . . ."

"Perhaps we will have another chance. . .in times to come." Jeremiah's gaze followed Sarah's hands as she shifted them to her lap.

"Perhaps," Sarah replied.

Jeremiah scooted his chair around so he could face her. "I am sure Bessie told you about the wonderful food the women provided that night."

Sarah glanced at Bessie, who sat with Sammy on the floor to help him stack blocks. "No. She only mentioned that Gemma sat with you."

"Well, let me see if I can do the supper justice." Jeremiah did not mention Gemma while he spoke of the roast pork, turkey, potatoes, and vegetables. He ended by saying he devoured several slices of apple, sweet potato, and mincemeat pies.

"You ate all that?"

Jeremiah patted his stomach. "It was enough to hold me for a week."

"I see. Perhaps I should throw a few more potatoes in the kettle to ensure we have enough stew for tonight," Sarah teased.

Bessie cleared her throat, and before Sarah knew it, Bessie rushed Sammy from the room.

Sarah's brow narrowed. "Did I say something wrong?"

"No. Bessie knows that I am about to tell you I cannot stay and eat tonight."

"You cannot?" Sarah felt as if every hope she'd ever dreamed was ripped to shreds and laid at her feet.

Jeremiah traced the line of her jaw with his gaze. "No. We. . .er. . .the militia has a campaign. I have to go with them."

"I see." Sarah did not know how much she had looked forward to seeing Jeremiah until he said he was not staying.

"Do you?" Jeremiah gazed at Sarah, memorizing her looks.

Her hair was twisted into some sort of fancy arrangement on the back of her neck. Her eyes followed his, as if she were trying to commit to memory what he looked like also. Gemma didn't look at him like this. Gemma looked at him with marriage in her eyes, no matter how many times Jeremiah told her that he was not interested.

"Yes, Jeremiah. Above all else, you must uphold your military obligations."

Pain clawed at Jeremiah's heart. He wanted to sit here with Sarah. To watch her as she cooked, or baked, or sewed, or performed one of the hundred other tasks women did in a household. He would give anything for that privilege, regardless of what he had promised after losing Jenny. There came a time when a man took what God sent, thanked Him for the gift, and moved on to enjoy life with that blessing by his side.

Jeremiah suspected that was why God kept him in uniform in Washington County. So he could heal Sarah's heart.

"When do you leave?" Sarah's words were hesitant.

Jeremiah shifted his tone so that it was more professional, more appropriate for the task that was about to take him away. If he kept his distance, it would be easier to say farewell.

"Tonight. I should be back by next Sunday. Certainly no later than Wednesday of the next week."

"Is it serious?"

"It relates to that earlier discussion we had about those Ohio settlements. Have you changed your mind about giving me information?"

"In a way." Sarah searched his face. "I can tell you that when I left the mission, there were almost two hundred people living there. Most of them were Delaware Indians, people I knew. We considered another settlement downriver our sister settlement. I think there were perhaps half as many there. They were Mohicans, but Christians."

"Thank you, Sarah. I have done some thinking lately. I should not have pushed you to tell me things you were not ready to talk about. Please accept my apology."

Sarah watched as Jeremiah rubbed his hands together, then she answered, "I should not have been so stubborn. I would have told you, only. . ."

"It is all right, Sarah. You did what you thought was best. That is all I hoped for."

Their eyes met and held.

"You will be careful?" Sarah whispered.

"It is the only way I do business, Sarah."

"Do you think it would do any good if I asked God to watch over you?"

"I think God is waiting for you to talk to Him, Sarah."

"I will then."

"I asked Him to guard you, too, Sarah."

Sarah gave Jeremiah one of the most beautiful smiles he ever saw adorn a woman's face.

"So many people think I no longer believe. Sometimes I

act like I do not, but you know what, Jeremiah? Somewhere deep inside me is the truth. When you come back, will you help me find it?"

sixteen

I don't believe Colonel Williamson actually wants us to do this. The entire territory seems to have gone mad. Protect me, Lord. Be with me now as You've never been with me before.

The petition's echo was Jeremiah's only comfort when his commander's flinty gaze turned on him. "Last chance, Major Stewart. We are waiting."

Jeremiah felt the cold penetrate his warmest jacket. He once had wanted to be like David Williamson—bold, well liked, able to make snap decisions. Not anymore.

Jeremiah met the commander's glare without hesitation. "I refuse to participate, sir."

"You cannot mean that, Major Stewart. I promoted you because you have the potential to be a great leader. These redskins scalped a family. We found the woman's bloodstained dress among their belongings when we searched their homes."

"Leaders do not always make popular decisions, colonel. I think someone talked them into accepting that dress as part of a trade."

The only proof Jeremiah had of that was the startled look on the Indian's face when one of the militiamen pulled the stained garment out of a basket.

"This is not their full contingent," Jeremiah added. "If it were, there would be more than this. These folks were run out of here last fall by the British commander at Fort Detroit. The ones here only came back to collect what was left of last year's harvest. They could not have made the attacks on our county because they were not here to do it. I tell you, they are innocent."

Shade found out more than just tidbits on his last ride. Sure it had been risky sending the courier into parts unknown. The payoff was that Jeremiah now knew another part of God's design for his life. He was to convince as many as he could not to participate in this act.

"They are murderers," Williamson insisted. "They must pay for their crimes." He pinned Jeremiah with an icy stare. "Do I need to remind you that you are now my second-in-command? You will do as you are ordered. Is that clear?"

Jeremiah thought back to the militia's arrival in this quiet Ohio valley. Colonel Williamson promised the Indians protection from the British and ordered them to surrender their weapons. Once they complied, he directed them to two cabins where they now awaited their fate. The background noise of men cleaning and loading weapons muted the hymns being sung by the prisoners not far away.

Regret surfaced in Jeremiah. There were so many things he should have done since taking over as the vice-commander. He would do what he could. Williamson had pushed Jeremiah around for the last nine months. Winning this argument would make Williamson furious, but it was the only one Jeremiah thought worth winning.

"I will not do it, sir." Jeremiah spoke loudly, trying to forget what he knew was bound to happen. "There are others who feel as I do also."

Silence lapped at the valley's edge, broken only by a wild animal scurrying through the brush. The other men in the company looked anywhere but at Jeremiah or Williamson.

"I will not allow you to do this," Williamson ranted, his chest heaving.

"You do not have the power to stop me, sir. You told me from the beginning that you would not press me into doing something I did not believe in."

"That applied to taking care of things like ordering weapons and such, and you know it. It certainly did not apply to this."

"This is what I will have no part in," Jeremiah asserted. "Nor will any other man who feels it is wrong to take a life. What you do not know, Colonel, is that I posted my resignation to Philadelphia last week. I am no longer a member of your militia, nor am I subject to your rules. There were other names on that letter, too."

"That is impossible. I would know if any of these men did not want to be here." Williamson glared at his group.

"You are never around," Jeremiah pointed out. He glanced at the soldiers. "Those who earlier indicated that they wish to stand down may form up over there." He pointed to a dip in the landscape.

Shade moved first. Thirteen others followed. They formed a ragged line of rebellion, their faces pale and lined. Jeremiah gave them high marks for upholding their convictions and not lowering themselves to the ranks of those who only wanted to satisfy the fright in their hearts.

"You cannot do this." Williamson fastened an icy look on the deserters.

"We can and we will, sir. This war began with rebels who sought the freedom to worship and who believed that they could make life better. Go ahead with your plan, colonel. We will pray for their souls, and for yours, for surely there is need of forgiveness here."

Williamson jerked on the reins of his horse. "You realize there will be a report on your insolence?"

Jeremiah nodded. He wasn't part of the militia any longer,

though he wasn't sure that would protect him. At least this way he could live with himself in the morning.

"I expect nothing less, sir. It is only fair to tell you that we also posted another letter before we left Washington County. It is a detailed summary to the president of the militia as to your plans for this mission."

Color drained from the colonel's face. He scowled at Jeremiah, as if unsure whether or not to believe him.

Rufe stepped forward, his stature as straight as an oak. "It is true, sir. I wrote it myself."

Jeremiah gave the clerk an encouraging smile before turning back to the commander. "Shoot me if it will make you feel any better, colonel. If I am gone, perhaps these men will rejoin your army."

"You are not worth wasting ammunition on," the colonel snapped. "Let us go, men. It is our duty to destroy these heathens before they destroy us. Axes to the ready!"

The men marched toward the cabins, their pace increasing as they topped a small rise. When they were out of sight, Jeremiah realized three more had joined his group, making eighteen total who stood on the side of right. How few they seemed next to the hundred who voted to attack. He had won this argument with the colonel, but his heart filled with sorrow that he had not convinced more to join him.

Forgive me, Lord, but I did my best.

Jeremiah gathered the men in a circle and asked them to join hands. "Let us pray."

He squeezed the hand next to his and did not continue until he felt the pressure returned from the man on his other side.

"Lord, grant them immunity from the final horrors of this life as they pass into Your love. Our Father who art in Heaven, hallowed be Thy name."

As the Ohio wilderness witnessed the destruction of a tribe who had only wanted religious freedom, Jeremiah and his following prayed throughout the night.

seventeen

"You came back." Sarah grabbed Jeremiah's arm and drew him into the home, shutting out the frigid evening air.

"I told you I would help you find God. I do try to keep my promises, Sarah."

Sarah ignored the burst of happiness that Jeremiah's presence created. She sensed that something bothered him. "Was your trip successful?"

"It did not go exactly as I would like. There are several things I must tell you, Sarah. But for now, I want to hear how you have been."

As she took a seat, Sarah tried to push away the nagging fear that squeezed her heart. Jeremiah settled into a chair across from her, pushing his sleeves up as if preparing for battle.

"You cut your hair, Jeremiah. I thought you were not going to do so until you were out of the militia. Oh, listen to me prattle. I have been fine, but I would rather hear about you, Jeremiah. Tell me everything."

"The whole thing may not be such a good idea."

Sarah's stomach sank. "I want to hear it anyway."

Jeremiah gave her a small smile. "Indulge me. There are some things I do not feel up to discussing just now."

Sarah didn't push Jeremiah as she might have when she first met him. "Then I will go first. Sammy said his letters from start to finish while you were gone. Bessie and Rufe are doing quite well themselves with reading."

Jeremiah's jaw showed some lessening of the tension he

146

had brought in with him. "I knew Samuel was a quick learner the first time I met him. Any man would be proud to claim him as his son. What else happened?"

Sarah's eyes glittered. "Captain and Bessie have studied with me."

"The Bible?"

Sarah nodded. "I know it was wrong to avoid God, but. . ."

"You are not ready to return yet," Jeremiah finished for her. "I understand, but I bet the angels stand ready to rejoice for your soul when you decide to do so."

"I do not know about singing; they might just hum."

Jeremiah laughed quietly. "Only you, Sarah. Only you."

"It has been quiet around here lately," she said. "Captain said he thinks the cold keeps the savages away. But what about you? The north wind was absolutely horrible here the other night. I wondered if you stayed warm and had enough to eat."

"I managed to survive. Quiet is good. I suppose if they do not send out detachments to look for rebels, that is a sign the militia is doing something right."

"Is that the only thing you care about, Jeremiah?"

"Not anymore."

"Not any—I do not understand."

"I am no longer a part of them."

"That is. . .good to hear," Sarah admitted.

Jeremiah spoke in a broken whisper. "As hard as I tried, I could not do what the colonel ordered. I kept thinking of you, Sarah. I knew you would never forgive me if I went along with the campaign."

A burst of happiness filled Sarah's heart. Jeremiah had thought of her while he was gone! She composed herself.

"I am the last person you should worry about," Sarah reminded him. "You should know that by now."

Jeremiah's voice was low and smooth. "I do, but there are some things in life I cannot control. One of them is that I worry about you."

"There is no need for you to do so," Sarah insisted.

Jeremiah stretched his hand out toward her. "I wish it were that easy. No matter where I go or what I do, Sarah, you push your way to the front of my heart."

"I find *I* can make myself do just about anything I wish," Sarah argued. "Just tell yourself I do not exist."

"Is that what you do? Tell yourself I am not a real person, with hurts and feelings?"

"Sometimes. It is safer that way."

❧

Later that night Sarah realized that she had not told Jeremiah the truth. No matter how she pretended, Jeremiah was very real to her. He felt pain, and, like Sarah herself, he needed someone to help him become whole. He professed to be God-fearing. God would not keep him warm on a winter night when howling winds forced their way through the chinking of cabin walls.

Sarah swallowed her discomfort. There she went, thinking that perhaps someday—years from now—there might be a man like Jeremiah who would love her.

❧

"Gemma, please," Jeremiah said. "We've gone over this too many times already. Your uncle and I did not agree. I took the only action that would allow me to continue living in line with God's Word."

Gemma dabbed at her eyes with a fancy handkerchief and sniffed. "Well, thank you very much, Mr. Stewart. I had such hopes for our lives as a couple. I suppose it is best that I find this out now. . .before you break my heart."

Despite Gemma's stoic words, Jeremiah knew he'd already

done that very thing. If only Sarah felt this way about him. But it was better that Sarah not feel anything for him other than friendship. Now that he had resigned his commission, it was only a matter of time before he headed back east to visit his pa and figure out what to do with the rest of his life.

⋟

"Tell me you are not serious," Bessie said as she watched Sarah beginning to pack her few belongings.

"You knew my moving here was not for the long term, Bessie. There is nothing here for me, no way to support Sammy. You and Captain have Lizzie. You should be a family and not have to worry about us."

"But where will you go, Sarah? Tell me that."

"I have a plan." Sarah neatly folded one of Sammy's shirts before placing it in her only trunk.

"Does that plan include coming back here someday?" Bessie's eyes overflowed with tears.

"I cannot answer that right now," Sarah replied. "It is time I move on and find whatever it is I am supposed to do with my life."

"Promise me you will speak with Jeremiah before you leave. I think he needs to know what you are doing."

"Jeremiah has Gemma, Bessie. I walked to the river yesterday to think things through. Gemma intercepted me there. She indicated that she and Jeremiah are. . .an item."

Bessie rolled her eyes. "But Jeremiah does not love Gemma. He loves you, Sarah. He has all along."

"Come on, Bessie, admit it. Your success at matchmaking this time has failed."

Bessie crossed the room and put her arms around Sarah. "If you are too stubborn to see what is in front of you, then I will not argue. I will miss you. You do not know how much help you have been. Thanks to you, I can read. Someday I will teach little Lizzie to do the same."

Sarah's eyes misted. "I am glad I gave you something that you will remember me by."

"But what will I give you? Wait! I know; I can read to you from the Bible to show you how well I can do."

"That would be nice." Sarah hoped she hid the commotion boiling inside her. There was no hope for her as far as Jeremiah was concerned. She did not think she was far enough in her journey back to God that she could bear to stay and see Jeremiah with Gemma.

"Let me pick something special," Bessie said, pulling Sarah's mind back to the present. "Meet me in the eating room."

Moments later, Bessie haltingly read from Psalm 103: " 'Bless the LORD, O my soul: and all that is within me, bless his holy name. Bless the LORD, O my soul, and forget not all his benefits: Who forgiveth all thine iniquities; who healeth all thy diseases; Who redeemeth thy life from destruction; who crowneth thee with lovingkindness and tender mercies.' "

"Are you listening, Sarah?"

"Yes." How could she not listen? The words pulled at Sarah and urged her to do the right thing, to return to her heavenly Father and accept His grace.

"I picked this verse because it says all I need to know about our Lord, Sarah. Only He serves as our ultimate protector, our source of comfort. God can heal your heart, Sarah, if you let Him. Is that not a wonderful thought?"

"Yes, it is. The words are just as you say. They combine hope, faith, and trust in a Supreme Being who accepts me just as I am, despite what I've done."

God can heal your heart, if you let Him. Bessie's words echoed in Sarah's mind that night as she tossed on her mat. God could heal her heart, but only if Sarah allowed Him to.

Why did she not take the last step toward believing?

&

Low-hanging clouds and a slight breeze made it feel colder than it was as Sarah headed toward the trading post. Jeremiah came from the other direction, and with the woods on either side, she had no choice but to speak to him.

They exchanged small pleasantries, and Sarah acted as if she were going to continue her walk.

"Sarah? There is something that I have to tell you." Jeremiah stuck his hands in his pockets.

Sarah's calm voice belied the depression in her heart. "You do not have to. Gemma cornered me the other day at the riverbank. I am happy that you have found someone to help you get over Jenny."

Jeremiah gave her a puzzled look. "How do you know about Jenny?"

"Bessie told me you loved her. That is all." Pain gouged Sarah's heart. Gemma, fortunate woman that she was, had lightened Jeremiah's burden.

"You told me that you wanted me to help you hunt for the truth," Jeremiah said. "We did not get a chance the other night, upon my return, to begin that journey. That is why I was coming to find you."

"I do not think you need to worry about helping me with that anymore. You have other. . .other things to tend to."

"But I promised I would. At least grant me the privilege of saying what I think."

Sarah nodded her permission.

"One thing I learned in dealing with Jenny's death is that a person cannot keep their grief locked up in their heart forever, Sarah. They never get beyond it if they do."

"You are simply luckier than most, Jeremiah. You happened to find someone who means something to you."

Tears threatened without warning. Sarah brushed them away. "I can keep my anguish to myself. No one but God will ever understand my feelings."

eighteen

Jeremiah watched Sarah turn and run back toward the Halls's. Unless she put her trust in God, he knew she would always search for something she would never find.

Jeremiah's rap on the door was too forceful, but he meant business, and it was not militia business this time. It took some doing, but Bessie helped him persuade Sarah to sit with him by the fireplace and continue their conversation.

"You have to share your burden, Sarah. That way it halves the grief."

Sarah looked as if she didn't follow his meaning. "You really want to know the truth?"

Jeremiah nodded. "We all make bad choices. It is part of God's way of teaching us to be better, to make us stronger."

Sarah stood. "Bad choices are indeed my problem, Jeremiah. If I had not insisted that Levi. . ."

Sarah's sobs sliced through Jeremiah like the flint head of an enemy's arrow.

"You keep looking for something to wipe away whatever it is you did, Sarah. Only God's grace can do that."

"His grace seems so far away, Jeremiah. I do not think I will ever feel happy and free again. Why is that?" The most ancient kind of hurt filled Sarah's eyes.

"I do not know, Sarah. I know I have been there, too. It is not easy alone. Just as you need God to help mend your heart, I need you." Jeremiah rose and wiped a tear from Sarah's cheek.

Sarah caught her breath. "What if I do not want you to need me?"

Jeremiah's voice held a note of disbelief. "I think you do want me to care, but you are so sure you might lose whatever you and Levi shared that you will not allow it."

"Levi was Sammy's father," Sarah pointed out.

"And you loved him."

"I still do."

"Do you? Or do you love the memory you have of him?"

Sarah's eyes clouded with uneasiness. "I do not want to forget him."

Huskiness broke Jeremiah's voice. "I do not want anyone to ask me to forget Jenny Townsend either. Look at Captain and Bessie. Both lost their mates, but they built a new life together. They know what it is like to lose, to have their dreams crumble into ashes."

"How did they survive? How did they put the past behind them and move on?"

"Sarah, are you asking how they freed their hearts to love again?"

"Yes."

"They gave God their hardships. They let Him restore their souls."

"How did. . .do you do it?" Sarah ventured.

Jeremiah studied her face. "At first I did much the same as you. I turned away from God. I grew bitter and spiteful."

"You are not. . .not that way now."

"I would be if I allowed my path to stray from that which is right. Now I keep God first, let Him lead me in the direction He chooses."

Sarah began to pace. "Does it help?"

"He is the only reason I can go on each day, Sarah."

Sarah stared into the fireplace.

Jeremiah spoke sincerely. "I am not good with fancy words, Sarah. Now that I am out of the militia, I do not even have a home. Thankfully, Rufe's father agreed to let me stay with them. I am just Jeremiah Francis Stewart, but I want you to be happy. I want you to care about me as much as I care about you."

"How can you say that, Jeremiah? Gemma said that you and she were going to wed."

"Gemma does not want to accept what I have told her all along. Now may I finish what I was saying?"

"Of course you may."

"I care about you, Sarah Lyons, but there are things I need to share with you about my past."

Jeremiah was uneasy about what he was about to say. Did he already regret announcing that he cared for her?

"I loved Jenny Townsend. She was everything I had wanted in a wife. She thought the world of me and would have made a wonderful mother for my children."

"So that explains why you keep coming here. You want children and I have one?"

"Let me finish. Jenny and I would have married if she had not taken a trip to visit her brother."

"What happened?" Sarah steeled her heart for his confession.

"Indians. One of our patrols found Jenny and her brother and buried them on the spot."

"I am sorry," she managed in a small voice.

"I am, too." Jeremiah sank into a chair and faced her. He shoved one shirt sleeve from his elbow to his wrist and back again, over and over. "But it is in the past, Sarah."

Sarah felt her poise dissolve. Jeremiah's loss almost matched hers. So many others also had lost loved ones. But they did not let devastation tear them apart. They learned to deal with their loss, then moved on. Was it possible she. . . he. . .they could do so together?

"I believe God put me here for more than one reason."

Jeremiah told her he had originally come to Washington County so that when they wed, Jenny could stay close to her ailing mother. "The only skill I knew was blacksmithing. I set up my tools and went to work. I never dreamed I would end up involved with the militia."

Jeremiah hung his head. Sarah's stomach clenched. What could she say to ease his pain?

"When I lost Jenny," he continued, "the whole world could have disappeared and I would not have noticed. I returned to my parents' home to live. That is when Bessie came home because she had lost her husband. She helped me see that things do not happen only because we make bad decisions. Things also happen because God has other plans for us. He prunes us so we will grow stronger, smarter, able to love more deeply the next time because we have lost so much."

Jeremiah wanted Sarah to stay with him for the rest of his life. How could he convince her? For just a moment he closed his eyes in silent prayer. *Lord, You never fail to deliver me from difficult situations, even though I sometimes think Your response is too long in coming. Look at me, Lord—I'm standing here trying to get this woman to reconcile her past so she can share my future. Sarah doesn't love me. What do I do now, Lord?*

"I am truly sorry that you lost the woman you loved." Sarah pressed a hand against her brow as if her head hurt.

"It took awhile for me to get over Jenny. For a long while I did not want to."

"What changed your mind?"

"You. The first time I saw you, I knew God had a purpose for bringing you into my life. I just never dreamed what it would turn out to be."

"That points out the major difference in our lives. You believed in God all along. I am just coming back to Him.

What if I take the wrong path someday? There is no way we could be happy, Jeremiah. I do not want to be a stone around your neck."

"Stones have their use," he commented. "They anchor, they hold, they lock in place. We could not have built some of the homes in this county without them, but I would never call you a stone, Sarah. You are too lovely to be something like that."

"What would you call me then?"

"I do not know. I can think of nothing right now that lifts you to the heights you deserve, Sarah. You do not think you are worth much to anyone except your son. That is not true. You taught Bessie her letters and helped her learn to read. You gave Rufe the chance to learn also. Who knows how many people your efforts will touch in the future because you cared enough to get involved today?"

Jeremiah wished that he had not started this discussion. No, that wasn't true. He loved Sarah. If he were to have any chance at her loving him, he must get her to the point where she could let go of Levi.

Jeremiah searched her face. "I cannot take away your pain, Sarah. Only God can do that. But you have to turn to Him. He does not help if you do not ask."

"It cannot be that simple. What if He will not listen to me or take me back?"

"God always listens, Sarah. Even through all those times when you were not looking at Him, He watched you. He has never given up hope that you would return to Him."

A frown marred her features. "You make it sound so easy, Jeremiah. It is not."

"I know. It is like crossing a river with your heart outside your body. You do not think you will ever get it back in place. I was at that point once. It takes courage and persistence to change. You have to really want it, not just for yourself, but for those around you, especially Samuel."

"Leave him out of this. He is an innocent child who lost his father. What if something were to happen to me? Then where would he go?"

"There are quite a few around here who would gladly raise him, myself included. He is a fine boy, one you should want only the best for."

"I do. That is why I came here, to try to make life better for him."

"There is only one sure way you can do that, Sarah, and you know what it is. But do not do it if you do not mean it."

Sarah closed her eyes briefly, interrupting the tears that trickled out. "But what do I say?"

"Just start talking. If you really mean them, the words will come." Jeremiah covered her hand with his and gave it a gentle squeeze.

"Lord?" The word sounded stilted on her lips.

How could one word have so much power? It was a question Jeremiah didn't think he would ever be able to answer.

Sarah started with a sob. "My burden—take it so that I may be free."

Jeremiah watched as Sarah struggled with her disclosure. Her eyes were ringed in red. She looked as if she had spent the past week crying.

What am I supposed to do, Lord? I know You put me here to help this woman, but what do I possess that will give her the peace she needs?

Jeremiah thought of the night sky he used to fall asleep gazing at on trips as a courier for the militia. The light of thousands of stars glowed softly, the twinkles spelling out a message he couldn't decipher. Suddenly he knew why God had provided that heavenly display.

"Sarah. I found something to compare you to."

"What?" She raised tear-stained eyes to meet his gaze.

"You are like a star. Despite the darkness that surrounds you, you shine, even as you continue your search for the perfection you know is out there. God put the stars in our heaven, Sarah. He is perfection. And peace. He is the only place you will find it."

"You said you would help me?" She stretched her hand toward him.

Jeremiah held back his smile, covered her trembling fingers with his own, and gazed into her eyes. "Go on. Let it out."

Once Sarah started, the echoes from her past spewed forth as if the earth rent a mountain and every bleak thing within escaped. Jeremiah hardened his heart against the surge of tenderness that engulfed him.

"I did something terrible," Sarah said, her throat closing around the words. "Levi and I ran away to marry. I never dreamed of what lay ahead, that he would. . .die before me. I am the only one left now, the only one to raise Sammy. Sammy deserves so much more, but I messed up his life. He deserves a father, and he might have had one had I stayed at Schoenbrunn."

Sarah's heavy sobs battered Jeremiah's soul, reminding him of his own process of grieving for Jenny. How many times had he held back his sorrow in the hope it would go away, only to find it growing by leaps and bounds with each passing day?

"Take it slow, Sarah. God will wait for you."

"God might," she whispered, "but what about you, Jeremiah Stewart?"

nineteen

"I will wait," Jeremiah assured her. "The weather changed early this afternoon; I think it may be warm enough for a stroll. Would you care to go with me?"

Jeremiah thought that the quiet and solitude outside would enable him to find the words he had not yet spoken.

Sarah nodded. On the Halls' porch, she pressed his arm and drew to a halt, gazing at him. Shiny tears glinted on her cheeks, giving her the appearance of fragility that Jeremiah knew was not part of her true character. He needed to see Sarah smile, to feel the spark only she could produce within his heart.

A renewed urge to replace Sarah's pain with happiness spilled through Jeremiah. *I can do all things through Christ,* he reminded himself, quoting from Philippians.

Jeremiah sighed. He still must tell Sarah what happened a week ago at a tiny mission in eastern Ohio, a deceptively peaceful setting where only the hills knew the truth of what the militia had done.

Jeremiah could never remember how to pronounce the name. He recalled that Sarah once called it "Ja-nadd-den." Shade had told him it was "Ja-nade-den-hut-ten," which he said was Dutch for "huts of grace."

Where was God's grace on March 7, 1782? Nowhere near Gnadenhutten, Jeremiah could vouch for that. He remembered the scene, and fear shivered up his spine.

I pray their souls are at rest in Your court, Lord. I pray You gave them peace and welcomed them with open arms. If there are any who deserve Your favor, it is those who were slaughtered in cold blood.

Sarah tugged at his sleeve. "What is it? You have mumbled to yourself for several moments."

"I have?"

"Yes. It must be something terrible."

"Sarah, I fear what I have to tell you may upset you."

Sarah drew a deep breath and glanced around for something safe to cling to. They might as well be standing on a scrawny patch of spring grass. From a distance, vague sounds penetrated her awareness—an owl, a loon, a sentry calling out "All is well."

"Perhaps it would be better if we go back inside, Jeremiah. Captain and Bessie might want to hear this."

"No. This is between you and me."

Sarah met his gaze. "Go on then. It will not be any easier if you delay."

"There has been a terrible tragedy at the Gnadenhutten Mission."

Wild fear engulfed her. Sarah stumbled, a reaction to the thought that eight years ago she and her sister lived only five miles away from there. But Jeremiah didn't know that. His militia had apparently been a part of this tragedy he spoke of. If she told him now that she had lived among those Praying Indians, what would he think of her?

Sarah schooled her features into a mask that didn't betray her terror. "Go on."

"Do you remember the last trip I took?"

She nodded.

"It was part of Colonel Williamson's plan that the militia raid that mission."

"Why would he assault a mission filled with Christians?"

"Williamson decided it was time to punish the ones he thought responsible for murdering the Wallace family."

"And?"

"He wanted to settle once and for all the question running through the minds of the people who voted him into office."

"I do not see how that applies to me."

Jeremiah narrowed his eyes. "If you have any doubt about my actions during the journey, I wrote everything down. I do not blame the militia for wanting to strike out at those who they thought were at fault, but that does not make it right."

"Did someone try to change their minds?"

His gray eyes darkened. "I did."

"But you said there has been a terrible tragedy."

"They would not listen to me, Sarah. Most of the men were too full of desire to get back at the heathens. They. . .they massacred them. All I could do was pray for their souls."

Massacred. The word settled inside Sarah like ice water. She couldn't bring herself to repeat it aloud; it was too bloody, too dirty. She knew most of those people. They were solemn Christians who left Pennsylvania years ago because whites kept tormenting them.

"I tried to prevent it, Sarah. I did the best I could."

"But. . .how many are gone?" Sarah wanted to know about the people at Schoenbrunn; her sister Callie, Levi's parents, Brother David, little Storm Killbuck. Memories of them singing praises to their heavenly Father filtered into her thoughts. Was it possible she had waited too long and would never see them again?

"At least ninety were killed, possibly more."

The time has come, Sarah realized. *I can't hide the truth from Jeremiah any longer.*

"Do you know any of their names?. . .I mean, of the ones who were killed?"

Please don't say even one I recognize, Sarah begged silently. *Please.*

"No. Some of us voted not to participate. We came back before the rest did. I had already tendered my resignation from the militia. Colonel Williamson did not know that until we were there and ready to begin the campaign."

"It is all so senseless, Jeremiah. Just like Levi's death. Someone reacted without thinking, did they not? Do you still claim God is in control of this world? And if He is, why did He not halt the slaughter of good people?"

"I do not know why, Sarah. But I do know this: I brought an eight-year-old boy back with me. He says his name is Abel."

Sarah grabbed Jeremiah's sleeve. "You brought an Indian child here? What do you think you are going to do with him?"

"Now that the militia has no hold on me, I am going to raise him to forgive those who took his family away."

"What makes you so sure you can succeed at raising an Indian child, Jeremiah? Sometimes I think you have no idea of what life is all about."

"I was going to ask you to marry me so we could raise him together, along with Samuel, of course."

Sarah's mouth gaped. "You were going to do what?"

"You heard me. I want you to marry me."

"Me?" Everything else Jeremiah said since he arrived was momentarily forgotten. Jeremiah wanted to marry her!

"Because you are the one person who can help Abel get over his anger." Jeremiah drew a deep breath. "You left that mission under less than perfect circumstances, giving little thought to those you left behind, right?"

"Yes, but why would you think I would willingly help you bring up a child who has no parents, Jeremiah?"

"Because you grew up without them," Jeremiah said. "You told me you were an orphan. That is why you are so protective of your son, and your heart. You know what it is like to be without hope, to be lonely, to be lost, to have no relatives around to help you. Is that not right?"

Sarah inhaled deeply. "Not exactly. I do have a sister."

"Why did you not tell me that before?"

She dropped her gaze. "I was afraid that if you found out, you would track her down and tell her where I was."

"Would it be so terrible if I had?"

"Callie would have. . .told you about me. . .about what I did."

"The past is the past, Sarah. It does not matter to me where you came from, or what you did. What matters is who you are now. The woman standing in front of me is the woman I love."

"There is still something you do not know," she said.

"Then tell me so we can move on, Sarah."

Jeremiah's encouragement did little to stem the feeling that if she admitted this one last bit, he would walk away, leaving her stranded again. But once she started, the rest of her story rushed from her in a torrent.

"I chased after the man my sister was supposed to wed. When Callie did not want Levi, I took him. And look what happened. I killed him—Sammy's father—because I was jealous of my sister."

Jeremiah let Sarah's tears drain until there were no more before responding. "Levi was a grown man. He could have chosen not to go from the beginning, Sarah. You told me he loved you. I think you are being too harsh if you blame yourself for his death."

Sarah stared at Jeremiah. Was he right? Had she blamed herself all along for Levi's passing? She ached inside, but it was a hurt that relieved the pressure she had put on herself for the last two years.

"But it is for Levi's death that I do not think God can forgive me, Jeremiah."

Jeremiah leaned toward her. "If you repent, God forgives, Sarah. He does not rank sin according to size, or depth, or the person involved. A wrong is a wrong, a sin is a sin. If you feel you were wrong, then ask God for His forgiveness. Do not ever think He cannot forgive; He is the only one who can."

"I hurt my sister. . . . It is all such a tangle! How will I ever sort it out?"

"Let God guide your path."

Sarah's tears ran freely. With Jeremiah as her guide, Sarah sought God's forgiveness. Emotions burned at her eyes, but she ignored the discomfort. Inside, for the first time in years, she felt cleansed.

"What if I slip someday, Jeremiah?"

"I will be there to help put you back on the right path."

"And will you help me find my sister?"

"You do not know where she is?"

"She was at Schoenbrunn when I. . .left eight years ago."

Jeremiah dipped his head slightly. "I went to Schoenbrunn just last month. No one lives there now but renegade Indians and British army deserters."

Sarah gave a cry. "I will never find her. I knew I should not wait so long to go back."

"I know someone who is fairly good at finding information," Jeremiah said. "Let me ask Shade to help."

"That is all well and good, Jeremiah, but what happens if he cannot? Then what will I do? I have to ask Callie for forgiveness or I will never know true peace inside." Sarah held her chin at a determined angle.

"We will not stop until we discover where she is."

❧

Jeremiah caught Bessie peering through the tiny window, her face filled with quiet joy. She'd known from the beginning that something good would happen when God brought together two people like Jeremiah and Sarah. Why hadn't he believed her?

"I think it is time to return to something I said earlier. I love you, Sarah Lyons. I have since the day I met you, though I was too headstrong to realize it. Now, one more time, because I will not ask again: Will you help me raise Samuel and Abel so that they see that love is the only emotion worth pursuing in this world?"

"Samuel Stewart?"

"He will never be mine, Sarah, but he will be ours. I promise. He can remain Samuel Lyons for the rest of his life if it will convince you to marry me."

"Sammy Stewart." Sarah gave Jeremiah permission to call her son by the favored nickname only she used. "And it is about time you asked, Jeremiah."

epilogue

"Howdy, neighbor!" A flock of cackling chickens accompanied the man's greeting. Behind him was a quaint, well-built log home. A musket was slung across his body. "What can I do for you?"

Sarah clenched her husband's arm. Now that they were here, she did not think she could go through with this part of their journey. They had first gone to Jeremiah's home, where Sarah spent a week getting to know his pa and Hazel, his father's wife. Before they left, Jeremiah and Pa resolved any lingering resentment over Jeremiah having been in the militia. Hazel was a delightful woman who insisted that they return and bring their sons with them.

As if he knew what she was thinking, Jeremiah held Sarah's hand and gave her an encouraging smile. He rolled from the wagon seat, holding his hands up to show he carried no weapons.

"We are looking for a woman known as Callie Troyer. We heard she lives here."

Beneath a wide-brimmed hat, worry creased the farmer's tanned face. He drew one hand along the stock of the weapon as if preparing to flip it to his shoulder and take aim. "Depends on why you want her."

"She is related to my wife." Jeremiah motioned to where Sarah sat on the wagon seat.

Sarah's mouth grew dry. The tension knotting her stomach for the last three miles solidified into a huge mass.

What if Callie wanted nothing to do with her? Thank

goodness they had left their sons, Sammy and Abel, with Captain and Bessie. *Their sons*—the words made Sarah smile despite the strain of the moment.

"That right?" The man perused Jeremiah. "Who might you be?"

Jeremiah introduced himself with a steady voice. Sarah bit her lip so hard she tasted blood.

The man raised the brim of his hat. A mass of tangled curls escaped. He was heavier than he'd been eight years ago, but Sarah would know him anywhere.

"Liope?" the man called over his shoulder. "Come on out. Your sister is here."

Liope? Sarah had never heard her sister called that before. A small eternity passed, long enough for Sarah to pray that God's will meant that all would work out.

"Josh?" The woman's voice was filled with concern. "I thought I heard you say my. . ." Her gaze traveled to Sarah.

"Sarah?" She shoved the toddler clamped around her hip at her husband. "Oh, Sare. It is you!"

Sarah met Callie halfway. Neither spoke. Their gazes held each other's, first cold with the memory of a long ago night, then warming with remembrance of all they shared as sisters.

"I had to come," Sarah croaked out. "I have to explain. . ." Words crowded her throat.

"Nothing is important except that you are here." Callie flung her arms around her younger sister. Sarah returned the embrace. Years of worry, wonder, and waiting blossomed in her eyes and made her unable to reply.

"I thought I would never see you again." Callie held Sarah away from her. "You do not know how many times I have prayed for this day, this moment, Sarah."

Sarah grasped Callie's hands. Callie wore the years well, and Sarah could tell Callie was happy.

Cackling chickens scurried nearby, scratching and paying no heed to the two women. Near the cabin, a small toddler cried out for "Mama."

"Your nephew Isaiah," Callie said, motioning to the youngster. "His sister, Sophie Ruth, is seven." She turned back to Sarah. "But what about you?"

Sarah related the events of the years that had passed. Having Sammy; losing Levi; finding Jeremiah.

"Our Lord?"

Sarah nodded.

"Then there is nothing else we need to say. If you have asked and received His forgiveness, I can do no less than give you mine."

Callie drew Sarah against her again. Sarah laid her head on her sister's shoulder in much the same way she had when they were younger. Peace settled within her heart.

It had been such a long trek—a long, winding journey much like Moses and his people undertook. They'd wandered through a desert; her trip involved a wilderness. Along the way she learned to trust, to need, and to accept help from others.

She had restored her faith, regained her sister, and healed her heart. Sarah lifted her head and looked toward Jeremiah. He stood beside Joshua. The two of them chatted as if they had known each other forever.

A verse from Psalms crossed Sarah's mind: *"A man plots his course, but the Lord determines his footsteps."*

She closed her eyes and leaned into Callie's embrace. Being independent was no longer important, Sarah realized. She was a child of the King. She could do almost anything alone if she had to. But she much preferred being loved by the people she loved most.

Captain and Bessie, who were adding another small bundle to their family.

Abel, the wisp of an Indian boy with his lisping way of calling her Ma-Ma, and who had formed an uncanny relationship with Shade, the messenger who pointed Sarah in the direction of her sister.

Sammy, who loved having an older brother and who was helping Abel learn to read.

Callie, who had spent as many days and nights as Sarah had waiting to be together with her sister again.

Jeremiah, the man she would walk proudly beside for as long as God gave her life.

Lastly, but most importantly, God. For without Him, Sarah would be no one, no matter who loved her here on earth.

A Letter To Our Readers

Dear Reader:

In order that we might better contribute to your reading enjoyment, we would appreciate your taking a few minutes to respond to the following questions. We welcome your comments and read each form and letter we receive. When completed, please return to the following:

Rebecca Germany, Fiction Editor
Heartsong Presents
PO Box 719
Uhrichsville, Ohio 44683

1. Did you enjoy reading *Healing Sarah's Heart*?
   ☐ Very much. I would like to see more books
      by this author!
   ☐ Moderately
      I would have enjoyed it more if _____
      _____
      _____

2. Are you a member of **Heartsong Presents**? Yes ☐ No ☐
   If no, where did you purchase this book?_____
   _____

3. How would you rate, on a scale from 1 (poor) to 5 (superior), the cover design?_____

4. On a scale from 1 (poor) to 10 (superior), please rate the following elements.

   _____ Heroine   _____ Plot

   _____ Hero   _____ Inspirational theme

   _____ Setting   _____ Secondary characters

5. These characters were special because_____

_____

_____

6. How has this book inspired your life?_____

_____

_____

7. What settings would you like to see covered in future
   Heartsong Presents books?_____

_____

_____

8. What are some inspirational themes you would like to see
   treated in future books?_____

_____

_____

9. Would you be interested in reading other **Heartsong
   Presents** titles?   Yes ❏   No ❏

10. Please check your age range:
    ❏ Under 18   ❏ 18-24   ❏ 25-34
    ❏ 35-45   ❏ 46-55   ❏ Over 55

11. How many hours per week do you read?_____

Name _____

Occupation _____

Address _____

City _____ State _____ Zip _____

American
DREAM

Journey with the immigrant settlers who made the United States a wonderful patchwork of common goals. Celebrate as love overcomes the tests brought on by a strange and untamed land. paperback, 352 pages, 5 ⁹⁄₁₆" x 8"

♥ ♥ ♥ ♥ ♥ ♥ ♥ ❤ ♥ ♥ ♥ ♥ ♥ ♥ ♥

♥ ♥ ♥ ♥ ♥ ♥ ♥ ❤ ♥ ♥ ♥ ♥ ♥ ♥ ♥

·······Presents·······

Great Inspirational Romance at a Great Price!

Heartsong Presents books are inspirational romances in contemporary and historical settings, designed to give you an enjoyable, spirit-lifting reading experience. You can choose wonderfully written titles from some of today's best authors like Peggy Darty, Sally Laity, Tracie Peterson, Colleen L. Reece, Lauraine Snelling, and many others.

When ordering quantities less than twelve, above titles are $2.95 each.
Not all titles may be available at time of order.

SEND TO: Heartsong Presents Reader's Service
P.O. Box 719, Uhrichsville, Ohio 44683

Please send me the items checked above. I am enclosing $_____.
(please add $2.00 to cover postage per order. OH add 6.25% tax. NJ add 6%). Send check or money order, no cash or C.O.D.s, please.
To place a credit card order, call 1-800-847-8270.

NAME _____

ADDRESS _____

CITY/STATE _____ ZIP _____